Th Frost

DRAGON DESCENDANTS
Book 4

FROM
USA TODAY BESTSELLING AUTHOR
J.L WEIL

CONTENTS

DRAGON DESCENDANTS

A REVERSE HAREM SERIES

COPYRIGHTS

A Dark Magick Publishing publication, July 12, 2019
www.jlweil.com

DRAGON DESCENDANTS

A REVERSE HAREM SERIES

WRITTEN BY J.L. WEIL

The Raven Series
White Raven, book1
Black Crow, book2
Soul Symmetry, book3

The Divisa Series
Saving Angel, book1.
Hunting Angel, book2.
Chasing Angel, book3.
Loving Angel, book4.
Redeeming Angel, book5.
Losing Emma, A Divisa Novella
Breaking Emma, A Divisa Novella

Luminescence Trilogy
Luminescence, book1
Amethyst Tears, book2
Moondust, book3
Darkmist, A Luminescenece Novella, book4

Beauty Never Dies Chronicles

Slumber, book1
Entangled, book2

Nine Tails Series
First Shift, book 1
StormShift, book 2
FlameShift, book 3
TimeShift, book 4

Dragon Descendants, A Reverse Harem Series
Stealing Tranquility, book 1
Absorbing Poison, book 2
Taming Fire, book 3
Thawing Frost, book 4

Stand Alone Novels & Novellas
Starbound
Ancient Tides, Division 14: The Berkano Vampire
Collection
Falling Deep, A Havenwood Falls High Novella
Ascending Darkness, A Havenwood Falls High Novella

DRAGON DESCENDANTS

A REVERSE HAREM SERIES

ABOUT THAWING FROST

The end is near. But will Olivia be able to save her dragons and the home she has come to love? Return to the Veil in the epic conclusion to the Dragon Descendants.

An unexpected reunion brings new possibilities to Olivia's quest of finding the dragon stars. She and the four dragons travel to Iculon, a kingdom as cold and brutal as its heir. Olivia might have lost the Star of Fire to the witch Tianna, but she isn't willing to give up. Not by a long shot.

Issik Westgard preferred a life of quiet and solitude until he met Olivia Campbell, the girl who found a way to thaw his frosty heart.

War threatens the Veil and all Olivia holds dear. She might not know what her future holds, but she's willing to take the witch down with her to save the four dragons she loves. Piece by piece.

Four dragons.

One headstrong heroine.
And a reverse-harem fantasy romance that could change the fate of a dying race.

THAWING FROST will transport fans of Twilight, A Shade of Vampire, and The Curse of the Gods to an enchanted world unlike any other.

Prepare for a unique spin on the lore you love, and an adventure that is as thrilling as it is unexpected.

Scroll up and BUY NOW to begin...
*Recommended for ages 17+ due to language and sexual content.

DEDICATION

This book is for readers.
I wouldn't be able to do any of this without you!
I FLOVE you!

ACKNOWLEDGMENTS

First and foremost, I want to thank Stephany Wallace for being more than an incredible PA and editor, but also being my cheerleader and friend. I wouldn't get through my edits without those comments that make me lol.

Another huge thank you to Allisyn, who constantly helps me grow in my skills as a writer. I really do take all your notes to heart, even if it seems as if I'd forgotten them.

I want to give a big shoutout to the YA Vets. You know who you are. This group is a resource I can't do without. Muawah!

And as always, a massive thank you to the readers and reviewers. You guys give me the encouragement to keep doing this and making me believe in my dreams.
I FLOVE all of you!

1

A ray of orange light cleaved through the darkness, as I stared at the wanderer in front of me, my mouth gaping.

Tobias?

The name rang in my head. This wanderer was the fifth dragon, the one Tianna's curse had supposedly killed years ago. How could that be? He was an old man, nothing like the four healthy and strong descendants flanking me.

"Tobias?" Jase called, his violet eyes a mixture of disbelief and suspicion. "Is that really you?"

I had no idea how they recognized their friend, under the white hair peppering his cheeks and chin. It covered most of his weathered face, leaving just the twinkle of his silver eyes visible under the hood.

Tobias nodded, and I swore his lips curved under the forest of hair. "It's been a long time," he confirmed in a deep, gruff timbre.

"How can this be? How are you here?" Zade asked, scrutinizing Tobias from head to toe as if he still couldn't believe it was true. The descendants weren't about to take his word for it, regardless of what their intuition was telling them.

"We saw you, your dragon bones," Kieran clarified, while the sun glinted off his green-flecked hair—it laid flat for once, brushed back by his fingers.

Drops of sweat slid down Tobias brow as he wiped it. He had to be miserable in this heat, and under that cloak. "She killed the dragon, but not the man. The aging spell wore off, and the years caught up to me in a matter of weeks."

"Why didn't you come to us?" Jase questioned, a hurt scowl marring his lips.

Tobias' features pinched in a wince, when a gust of sandy wind hit his face. "As an old man? What could I possibly do to help you? I have no powers. No kingdom. Nothing to offer." Sadness flickered in his dove gray eyes. He'd lost everything. "I'd have only been in your way."

"Why would that matter?" Kieran challenged. "You're our friend, our brother."

A burdened sigh left Tobias' chest. "I couldn't leave my lands, even if the witch had destroyed them."

The Nameless Lands. They had once been alive, a place of beauty and life. Now they lay barren and void of life, except for Tianna and her army of warriors.

"You saved me," I reminded. "I wouldn't have escaped the witch's prison if it hadn't been for you."

Tobias's eyes scanned over the scar that ran along my cheek—a nasty gift from my time captured by the witch. "I'm glad to see you made it safely to the castle."

"I wouldn't be here if it wasn't for you. If there is anything I can do to repay you…" My words faded with the weight of truth.

I owed Tobias my life. My spine rocked with a shudder to even think of what else Tianna might have had in store for me. Would I still be in chains? Locked in the box of darkness? Would I have gone insane by now? I banished the thoughts from my head and shifted my body closer to Issik, who was nearest to me. His coolness gave me a reprieve from the sweltering heat of Crimson.

A curt nod was Tobias only answer.

Instinctively, Issik's fingers went to the small of my back, guiding me to lean into him, but he kept his gaze centered on Tobias. "Why have you come out of hiding now?" There was nothing friendly about Issik's tone.

I wondered the same thing. What made him risk the witch finding him? He had remained hidden for years. Perhaps she had discounted the old man, no longer considering him a threat. From what I knew of the wanderer, that was a very dumb move on her part.

Tobias's eyes narrowed a tad at Issik's protective gesture before they shifted, landing on me. "I have something... for you."

"For me?" I echoed, my brows pinching together. What could he want to give me?

Tobias nodded. "I know you're tired, and it has been a trying night. Meet me in two days, after you've rested, and before you travel to Iculon."

Jase stepped in front of me, and the maneuver wasn't lost on any of us. He would protect me, even from someone who had once been a friend. "Why should we trust you?"

To some degree, it was unnerving that Tobias knew of our movements and plans, but by process of elimination, it would only make sense we'd be heading to Iculon to recover the Star of Frost—the last dragon stone.

"You shouldn't trust anyone. The witch has eyes everywhere," Tobias warned, although we'd figured out that much on our own. "I don't expect you to blindly follow me, but can you afford not to come if it could mean destroying the witch? I have something in my possession that will aid you in your quest. It isn't wise to speak of it."

His gaze took to the skies, just as a gust of wind howled through the valley between the two lands. His fear of being overheard or watched was valid. Tianna did have spies all around us, and magic to see where her spies could not.

Meanwhile, Zade was monitoring Tobias's every move. I couldn't decipher if they were happy to see him, or wary of their friend. Maybe both. "What aren't you telling us?" he demanded.

Tobias lips curved into a tentative smile. "Come and I'll show you."

"Where?" Jase asked, his tone neither soft nor gentle. At that moment, he was every inch a dragon warrior with flaming violet eyes.

Tobias didn't so much as flinch, he himself having been a fearsome dragon. "At the border between these lands and Issik's kingdom. Dawn. She moves more freely during the night."

The four dragons shared a look, something passing between them that neither Tobias nor I were a part of. "We'll be there," Jase agreed.

"Until then," Tobias breathed, lifting his wooden staff to take a step back.

"Tobias, wait," Kieran called.

The wanderer paused and glanced up from under his hood, those silver eyes lit with question.

"Will you not come with us? Will you not join our fight? We are your brothers."

Not in blood, but in every other sense of the word they were. My heart cracked a little at the hope in Kieran's voice. I had no idea how they were feeling about seeing their old friend, knowing he was alive, but so frail, and without his power of persuasion.

Traces of remorse shone through Tobias's expression. "I can't. My place is here." His gaze indicated the barren land sprawling behind his back. "I will help with what I can, but I won't leave my kingdom. Not until this body has taken its last breath."

Jase bowed his head ever so slightly. "As you wish."

Issik's fingers fisted at the small of my back. "Let it be known that if you double-cross us, or if you harm Olivia in any way, I won't hesitate to give you that death you so desire."

I swallowed at the icy sharpness in Issik's words, glad I wasn't at the receiving end of the warning.

Yet, Tobias's eyes glimmered with amusement. "You haven't changed at all, old friend. I would be disappointed if you had." He gave Issik and the others a tip of his head, before he turned and hobbled off into the grainy air of the Nameless Lands. Within minutes, his outline was blurred by the winds of sand.

I wasn't looking forward to the journey back to Crimson castle. I wished we could willowphase. Perhaps the descendants should consider having a goblin, or two, in servitude in their kingdoms. It would make traveling a hell of a lot quicker and easier. I didn't mind flying, but this walking business... not for me, especially in my current state of sheer exhaustion. My legs strained to keep me upright, stumbling with nearly every step. I could no longer feel my feet.

"Come here, before you fall on your face," Jase murmured in annoyance.

He got no struggle from me as he lifted me into his arms. I swore I spent almost as much time being carried by them, as I did flying on their backs. I wrapped my arms around his neck, a frown taking over my lips. "What took you so long?" I muttered, stifling a yawn.

A low chuckle escaped his lips. "Pardon my thought-lessness."

Soon, it became difficult to keep my head up, so I gave in, resting it between his shoulder and neck. "I'm not as helpless as you think," I declared, wincing at how weak my voice sounded.

Jase's face tilted slightly toward me, and the wisps of his breath touched my lips. "You were never helpless, Cupcake." His golden chest glistened in the sun as the first rays of morning crested the foothills.

"I missed you," I murmured, though I didn't need to tell him why I had.

Since the attack on Wakeland, Jase had more or less checked out, his anger becoming a living thing inside him. Not having him around had been lonely, which was odd since I was rarely ever alone, but I had missed him all the same. Tremendously so.

Smugness tugged at the corners of his mouth. "Is that so?"

"Yes. Believe it or not, I need you in my life."

With my confession, the drumming of his heart became a little faster under my palm. "Good, because you're stuck with us. You've become vital to my life."

His words made my breath catch. After a night like we had, I needed to hear I was still important, that they still cared for me as I did them. My eyes drifted to where Kieran, Zade, and Issik walked a few feet in front of us, talking amongst themselves. I couldn't hear what they were saying, but seeing them together had me thinking about what happened tonight—what we had gained... and lost.

"I'm so sorry," I whispered, tears of guilt and remorse dampening my eyes.

Sensing the sadness that hit me in mounting waves, Issik looked at me over his shoulder.

Jase stilled. "For what?"

"I lost the Star of Fire," I whispered, my shoulders sagging in defeat. My body might have healed from Tianna's torture, but I bore internal scars that still ached.

Failure.

I felt as if I had failed them. I hadn't been strong enough to protect the star. Tianna took it from me, and it almost cost me my life.

Jase's lips grazed over my cheek as he leaned closer. "You have nothing to apologize for. Nothing. You did not fail. What you did—standing up to her like that—took guts. You should be proud of yourself. I know that I'm proud of you."

Emotion clogged my throat, impeding my ability to say anything in response. How could he not hold me responsible for losing the star? But he didn't. I could see it in his star-flecked eyes. "I'm going to get it back," I managed to say. If it was the last thing I did, I would return the star to its rightful home. It belonged to Zade, and I wouldn't stop hunting for it, even long after the curse was broken.

Jase's powerful chest heaved an exhale. "I believe you. As much as the idea cripples me with fear—you against the witch—you might be the only person who can take the stone from her. I don't like it, but it is not my place to interfere with fate. If you were meant to recover the Star of Fire, I won't stand in your way. I will stand beside you. Always."

I rubbed my cheek against his, my arms tightening around his neck. "Thank you." I never wanted to let go. His trust in me melted my heart. Because of his confidence, I could find the courage to keep moving forward.

My Dragons gave me purpose. They gave me a home. And most of all, they loved me.

The faint scent of honeysuckle and burning leaves floated in the air, and my eyes closed.

I must have dozed off, because the next thing I knew, I was being tucked into bed—a soft blanket draped over me. Under hooded lashes, I stared up at Jase, now perched on the edge of the bed.

His tender fingers swept strands of hair away from my face. "Your eyes…" he murmured.

I blinked, opening my eyes a bit wider, the wonder in his voice pulling me further away from the haze of sleep. "What's wrong with them?"

Shadows crept over his features. "They are… glowing."

My nose wrinkled. Was that all? From the expression on his face, I thought that I'd perhaps gained a third eye on my forehead or something equally as dramatic. "I take it that's a bad thing?"

His thumb glided along the column of my neck, leaving behind tingles in its wake. "I wouldn't say bad, just different for a human."

News flash: I doubted I was only human anymore. I was becoming less and less the girl I'd once been. "I'm not so sure I am still human," I replied, voicing my thoughts.

"How does the prospect make you feel? To be something different, someone capable of magic?"

I chewed on my bottom lip. "Tired. And unsure of myself," I admitted, pausing for a moment to ponder if I should tell him about the other thing that had happened tonight. Picking at a thread on the blanket, I forced my eyes upward. "When Tianna touched the star, her power passed between us. I think I took a piece of her magic."

Worry coiled in his eyes, before he shielded them with a blank slate. "Interesting. As much as the idea frightens me, it could be something we can use against her. She won't be happy you stole her power, which puts an even bigger target on your back. You're sure that's what happened?"

Rubbing at my wrists, I thought back to those seconds when Tianna and I had been ensnared by the star. The strange tang in the back of my throat. The tingles that coursed through my veins, were so different than the fire that had raged alongside it. Tianna's power was dark and alluring.

"Anything is possible, but I…" My voice trailed as I gathered my thoughts. "I can feel it," I admitted, shifting on the bed so I could lay a hand in between my breasts. "Right here. It's like a little seed of magic has rooted inside me, sprouting into something more. Something dark." I risked glancing up, nervous of what I might see in his face.

Would he see me as tainted? Would he think I was wicked?

"Your power grows stronger. She felt it tonight, and that will make her think twice about going head to head with you next time."

Next time. The words echoed in my head. It was inevitable the witch and I would meet again, regardless that I wished otherwise.

The Star of Frost was out there, waiting for me. *Like calls to like*—that's what the women in white had told me. With the powers of tranquility, poison, and fire swimming inside me, I hoped locating frost wouldn't be difficult, but I also prayed it would be enough. After the loss of the fire stone, I was uncertain how that affected the descendants' curse. Would the portal be opened? Would the descendants be free? Or must I have the stones in my possession?

Tianna stealing the stone was a setback, but only time would tell how big or small that misfortune was. I had every intention of stealing it back and returning the star to Zade, the rightful heir.

Jase leaned down and kissed the tip of my nose. "Now, get some sleep." He moved to pull back, but I placed a hand on his forearm, and his brows lifted. "Do you want me to…"

I knew precisely what he was offering. "No tranquility."

Although, after everything that had happened, it was a tempting proposition. I didn't want the nightmares that would surely come. I didn't want to think about my eyes glowing, or what other changes I could expect from my body. I didn't want to think of anything at all.

"Stay with me," I whispered.

Jase didn't hesitate as he pulled back the quilt and settled in alongside me, the bed groaning as it adjusted to his weight. "Always," he murmured, opening an arm for me to curl into.

There were undoubtedly a million things he needed to discuss with the other descendants. He was probably dying for a shower. His skin still faintly smelled of smoke and sweat—which I found oddly comforting—but he put all those things aside to hold me as long as I slept, because I asked and it was what I needed.

He calmed me in a way no one else could.

2

Issik paced in front of the onyx fireplace in Zade's study the following morning, his movements cold and sharp. His blond hair was unbound, dangling to the scruff on his chin. The gray tunic he wore stretched over his broad chest.

"Are we seriously considering meeting with Tobias in the Nameless Lands?" Zade growled from behind his massive ebony desk.

"We don't know anything about him, or why he's been hiding all these years. For all we know, this could be a trap. He could be working with Tianna. He *is* in her territory," Issik pointed out to us.

From my position on the chaise, my eyes trailed his movements from one side of the hearth to the other. "Actually, no. Tianna invaded *his* territory. Did you forget that he orchestrated my escape?" I reminded them, not sure why I felt the need to defend Tobias. It wasn't as if I knew the old man well.

Issik threw a glance in my direction that felt like chips of ice. "He could have helped you to gain our trust."

"There is no point in us snapping at each other," Jase snarled at Issik from the chair across from mine. A low wooden table sat between us, with books and parchment scattered on top of it.

I stifled a snort at his tone. That was rich. He was right there with the others, barking and puffing out his arrogant chest.

"Do any of us believe Tobias could have sold us out?" Shadows from the firelight danced over the side of Kieran's face. He leaned against the wall near the heart, arms crossed over his forest green shirt.

Sorrow doused the fire in Zade's eyes. "Not the Tobias we once knew, but Tianna is capable of turning even the most loyal of friends against one another. He has been out there in the Nameless Lands, alone, for years. We can't be sure the witch hasn't corrupted him, but we also can't disregard this meeting. If Tobias knows of something that could help destroy Tianna, I think it is worth the risk."

"I agree," Jase sighed. "I don't like it, but we can't continue to let her terrorize our kingdoms." It was evident in his expression that he was thinking about his own castle, and the spell now preventing him from entering his home.

My heart bled for him, for the people stuck inside.

Issik's jaw clenched. "She has half of the creatures in this world under her spell. It would be naive of us to think the same couldn't be done to one of us."

Zade's hand raked through his slicked back, coffee-colored hair. "If that's true, why hasn't she already pitted us against each other?"

"Because she needs you," I answered plainly. "It is the

13

only way she can get the stars. Her goal has always been to gain the power of the dragon stones."

The air simmered with rage. Four dragons each expelling their hatred for one woman simultaneously. From across the room, Kieran's eyes blazed a bright green. "I'm going to peel the skin from her body, and poison her slowly."

"Knowing Tianna, she might thoroughly enjoy the experience," Jase coolly added.

I pressed my lips into a thin line, understanding Kieran's need for revenge and justice. "We need to go to the Nameless Lands. I don't know him as you guys do, but it feels important." I couldn't give them a solid reason. I only had intuition and this tug in my chest telling me to go.

I was asking them to trust me.

Four sets of eyes studied me with a mixture of intrigue, confusion, and doubt. "It's settled. We leave in the morning," Jase decided, giving the final word on the issue.

I stood on what seemed like the edge of the world. Wind and sand spun out before us, making the visibility dodgy. Red and gold danced on the horizon as morning broke over the land. We stood atop a dune, overlooking the barren desert that was the Nameless Lands. Even with the dawn's breeze, the air was thick, causing the thin material of my clothes to cling to my body. My lips were dry as I licked them.

We had stayed within Crimson until we reached the southern point of the kingdom, where it crossed over into the Nameless Lands. In the distance, snowcapped mountains to the northeast rose up to the sky.

Crossing borders into new territories never failed to awe me. It was so different from Earth, where the lands gradually merged into one another. In the Veil, the lines were more definite. I could feel, smell, and immediately see the difference. It was kind of similar to teleportation.

Although Crimson was visible over my shoulder, it looked as if I was peering through a mirror into another world. Gone was the sweltering heat of the previous land, replaced by a dry warmth. The air was grainy here, and the ground felt different, heavier.

Howling winds and our shuffling steps through the sand were the only sounds. I buried my face deeper into the scarf wrapped over my nose and mouth—my protection to keep the dust from invading my lungs.

The Nameless Lands was my least favorite place of the Veil Isles. Endless miles of lonely earth stretched out before us. Not to mention the memories of being imprisoned here. I hated the fear that coursed through my blood, the urge to run, the scream held back in my throat. As if I needed a reminder of the suffering I'd survived, the scar on my cheek tingled.

My hand rested on the hilt of the dagger strapped to my thigh. The weight of it gave me a small amount of security. Jase, Zade, and Issik were glaring in opposite directions, searching for any sign of Tobias, or danger of a magical kind. Kieran flew overhead, a lookout in case Tianna decided to cause trouble. Being this close to the mountain she used as her home was a risk. His shadow drew circles over the ground.

We were all in place, waiting for the former dragon to show.

A cut of muscle shifted under Issik's shirt. "If he doesn't appear in five minutes, we're out of here."

I rubbed at my chest. The blood inside my heart pumped harder the farther we traveled into the Nameless Lands.

Where is he? I silently asked, scouring the horizon for any sign of movement. I loathed being in the Nameless Lands. *Run. Run. Run,* my mind begged. I had to push aside the desire to flee, and steady my breath.

"He'll show," Jase stated with certainty.

"He better, if he knows what's good for him." Zade's nostrils flared. "I'll track his ass down and drag him here myself."

"I'm right behind you," Issik muttered, his eyes becoming sharp slits.

The three of them circled me, each taking up a similar stance—arms crossed, legs slightly apart. Their bodies made a shield, blocking a large part of the wind and sand from reaching me—a clever maneuver on their part, though restlessness licked the air, making me tense.

Seconds later, Tobias appeared out of thin air with a little green goblin at his side.

Willowphase. Of course, he would teleport, but I couldn't help but wonder if Tianna was able to track the use of magic. Was it a good idea for him to be teleporting around the Nameless Lands with her presence so near? Would she show up, magic blazing? An army surrounding us?

Panic clawed at my chest.

Issik nodded toward me, a gesture I realized was

intended for Jase, who weaved his fingers through mine instantly. A steady stream of calm flowed into me, and I sighed.

"Took you long enough," Zade bit out, unfolding his thick arms.

"Some things can't be controlled," Tobias replied cryptically, but his features appeared tired. The goblin peered up at him, concern flaring in his beady black eyes. I'd put money on this goblin being the same one who broke me out of my imprisonment, but I couldn't really remember him.

"We came as you asked. What is it you have?" Jase prompted, wasting no time in getting to the point. "None of us want to linger here, and we don't have time to squander."

Tobias held Jase's stare, his expression unreadable. "This." He pulled out an object from the lining of his black cloak, opening his palm for us to see.

I gasped, my heartbeat thundering in my ears.

Jase whistled through his teeth.

Issik glowered—nothing unusual about that.

And Zade's dark eyes widened. "Father above," he muttered.

A stone, identical to the other three I'd found sat nestled in Tobias's hand. It was a beautiful amber color and it gleamed like the sunrise at our backs, but something was different from the other stars—it lacked its spark.

Was I actually seeing what I thought? Could this be...

The Star of Persuasion?

"Where did you find that?" I asked Tobias, stepping forward to get a closer look, but a hand landed on my shoulder, and the sudden chill that radiated down my arm clued me to Issik's presence.

Tobias's eyes darkened. "I've spent years searching my kingdom, hiding from the witch, and flying under her radar. There is no part of these lands I've not touched. The *where* isn't important."

"How do we know this isn't some kind of trap, a spell from the witch herself?" Issik challenged, his hand still firmly resting on my arm.

The stone looked very real, but I understood his hesitation and distrust.

"I'm an old man, with nothing else to lose," Tobias reminded. "Before I die, I would like to know that I did something to save the home I love. I want to see it returned to its former glory, and I will do everything these weak bones will allow to make it so."

I was unable to look away from the stone, my eyes drawn to it, and yet, I waited for a kernel of recognition to flicker in me. However, the power of the other stones inside me, didn't pulse or thrum with excitement at their reunion with their long-lost companion. No desire to touch it whispered in my ears. So strange. It was as if there was very little life left inside of it—if any at all—and that nearly made me call Tobias a fraud.

Yet, as I opened my mouth, I felt it—the tiny sputtering of magic.

A speck pulsed at the center of the stone, so small that I almost didn't see it with my human eyes. It could have easily been mistaken for a trick of the sun. "What did you do to it?" I asked softly, lifting my gaze to meet his.

Tobias's sharp eyes studied me with intent from under his hood. "You're able to sense the lack of power?"

Still waiting for him to answer my question, I nodded.

His tall frame shifted, as the glint in his eyes focused on me. "Its power is gone. It died with my dragon, but I thought it might serve you in your quest." He offered the Star of Persuasion to me. "Take it," he insisted.

I waited to see if the descendants were going to object. My head angled to the side, and I regarded the stone again before I moved to grasp it. Issik didn't stop me, instead, his hand slid from my shoulder, letting me go.

The stone was neither cool nor warm, but a neutral temperature as it touched my fingers. A low hum murmured in my blood, so faintly that I wondered if I was only imagining it, wishing for it. The power of persuasion —what a dynamic gift. The idea both thrilled and frightened me. I flipped it over in my palm, rubbing its smooth surface. Up close, what looked like winds of sand swirled through the crystal's veins. "I'm not sure its power is gone completely." My voice was low, muffled by the scarf and carried away with the wind. I shook my head. "It's so faint."

Jase, Zade, and Issik gathered around me. Did they feel anything when they looked at the stone? From the scowls marring their faces, I guessed not.

"If there is even a crumb of power left in the star, I wish you to have it," Tobias confessed. "You've been chosen by the dragon stones. It is you and you alone who shall wield the power and join the dragons. The curse is nearly broken, but your fight won't end there."

Kieran's shadow passed over our heads, blocking the dawn's rays for a brief moment. My fingers closed around the stone. "Thank you." Pulling the scarf down from my face, I offered him a smile.

"Don't thank me yet." A ghost of a smirk curled under his beard, but it didn't last long. "It was fate our paths crossed, Olivia, Keeper of the Stars, and Savior of Dragons. You are meant to save this world, to save *them*." With the words, I could have sworn regret and sadness flickered in his eyes.

I swallowed the lump of emotion that sat in my throat. "I'm sorry I wasn't here before… to save you." My apology was sincere.

He nodded, sinking further into his cloak. "Protect her. Protect the stones," he urged the descendants, and grabbing the goblin's hand, they vanished from our sight.

A thump sounded behind me, followed by a gust of wind and a looming shadow. *"Someone want to tell me what that was all about?"* Kieran asked in our heads.

"It's time to go," Jase ordered.

Despair wormed its way into my belly. What Tobias said about Tianna's torment not ending with the opening of the portal to this world struck a chord inside me. We had come so far, and yet we had so much left to battle.

3

Upon our return to Crimson Keep, the castle was a flurry of activity as the staff prepared for our departure tomorrow.

The stone made its way around the room, each descendant taking the time to inspect the glossy amber crystal. Jase held it up to the window, shifting it with the light streaming through the glass. "Nothing happened when you touched it?" he asked.

Candles flickered along the mantel, which had been lit by Zade, while I tucked my legs underneath me on the couch. "No. At least not like the others. It was obvious when the surge of magic flowed inside me from each stone." The descendants each had sensed the transfer of power identical to theirs.

Perched on the coffee table in front of the couch, Kieran leaned toward me. "But you still believe there is a trickle of power left inside?"

I nodded, taking notice of how his light gray tunic stretched across his broad chest. "I do. I can't explain it, but maybe if we had the other stones, then this one would come alive again," I suggested, unsure where my brain had plucked the idea from exactly.

My thought sparked something in Jase, who moved away from the window to sit on the couch beside me. His long legs stretched under the low table. "That's an idea worth exploring another day." He passed the stone to me.

"Until then, we need to keep it somewhere safe," Zade confirmed.

The stars had been stashed in their perspective kingdoms, hidden away from Tianna. Not even I knew where the descendants had chosen their hiding places to be, except for Zade's. I offered the Star of Persuasion to him. "Until we recover the Star of Fire," I said, "you'll keep it hidden." It felt right to give him Tobias's stone. To keep the stars on us could be devastating—a single attack from Tianna and we could lose everything.

For a few seconds, Zade just stared at the stone, considering it. "It should stay with you," he concluded, lifting his eyes to mine. His fingers closed around my hand to secure the star in my palm. "It's where it belongs."

No one objected.

So be it. "I will keep it safe," I vowed, pressing my hand to my heart, and I swore the stone pulsed once, like a sigh of relief. My eyes drifted to Issik in the corner of the room. He'd been quiet since we'd come home—unusually so, even for him. I'd nearly forgotten he was there. His distrust of Tobias lingered like a dark aura around him.

"What Tobias said about the fight not being over even after the curse is broken, do you think it will come to war?" I asked, looping my arms around my drawn-up knees. My golden hair fell, framing my face. The stone was still in my right hand, and I had no intention of letting it go.

Jase's eyes churned with burdened thoughts. "All this time we've searched for the one to break the curse. We had foolishly believed your blood would save us. As the years passed, our hope of ever being freed seemed like a dream. Then we learned the blood was only a small portion of the cure. Tianna is cunning, masking her true desire for the stars with some ridiculous curse."

"The origins of the dragon stones has always been a closely guarded secret, held only by the founding kings of the Veil. Some legends claim the gods once lived with us in the Veil, and other worlds like ours. They gifted those worthy with magic, and thereby mystical creatures were made—dragons, witches, faeries, trolls, nymphs, and so on."

Issik's deep, cool voice was hypnotic, like a bedtime story on a cold winter's night.

"But magic comes with a price. Some abused their abilities, wanting and demanding more from the gods. It's never a good thing to demand anything from an immortal. When the gods bestowed the stones to the five dragon kings, they enchanted the crystals to harness their abilities, and the kings crafted them into different weapons of their choosing."

Jase's face grew solemn. "I don't believe any of us want war, but if a fight is what Tianna is after, we'll give her one."

"When we get to Iculon, it might be wise to do some reading on the stars," Kieran suggested. "Most of what we know about them comes from stories passed down through the generations."

I was looking forward to seeing Issik's castle, but the cold temperatures I could do without.

"What will you do if your full dragon powers aren't restored once the curse is broken?" I was asking all the tough questions, but someone had to do it. "Will you be able to defeat her?"

Jase rested his head on the back of the couch, huffing. "My ego says we could without question. There was a time when a witch of Tianna's skills never would have stood a chance against a single dragon, let alone four of us. But the circumstances have changed, and we need to accept our current limitations. Though, even if our abilities are only a fraction of what they once were, it won't change my heart or my drive to kill the witch. We'll find a way. *That* you can be certain of."

I trusted them with my life, so did everyone who lived here. Snuggling deeper into the couch, I stared at the candles flickering over the fireplace. A feeling of dread swept through me. Tianna would stop at nothing to gain the power she desired. It was no longer just about breaking the curse. She would come for me—for the stars, and the power they entrusted to me.

I knew it.

Tianna knew it.

But did the descendants know?

The four of them continued to strategize, and plan for the upcoming travel to Iculon. I was lost in my own thoughts and theories, none of which I hoped were true, but there would come a point when I would have to face my future, whatever that may be.

It might have been five minutes or an hour after my

mind wandered off, but the mention of my name refocused my attention on the conversation.

"We're going to need to get Olivia outfitted for the journey tomorrow." Kieran winked at me.

"I'll have Juniper see to it," Zade agreed.

My fingers twined together, tightening around the star. Tomorrow we left for Iculon—the coldest kingdom in the region. I was as ready as I'd ever been.

A snow-kissed breeze fluttered over the tip of my nose while we flew, and my cheeks grew red as I bristled at the cold of Iculon. I snuggled deeper into my hooded cloak, the navy blue velvet fabric felt soft on my face. It was decided I would be flying with Zade into the snowcapped mountain region. His warmth would keep me from freezing, and protect me against the blistering winds that whistled through the quiet land.

After crossing through a corner of Jase's kingdom, the unmarred blue sky transformed into a smoky gray, marking the edge of Iculon. The initial cold had stopped the air in my lungs, but the shock had soon given way, allowing me to breathe in the chilled mist. I'd never tasted air so crisp and pristine. Snow covered every inch of the ground, blurring the lines of where the mountains stopped, and the flat land began.

Zade crested a mountain, and on the other side, a lake of sheer ice spanned for miles. Crystals of light aqua sparkled like jewels under the frozen surface. He dipped down, sensing my amazement and wish for a closer look.

His expansive, dark red, almost black wings sliced through the air with ease.

Holding on to his scaled neck, I peered over his shoulder to look down at the wondrous lake. Our reflection glanced back at me—a rider on a majestic red dragon. "It's beautiful," I whispered in awe.

"Don't let its beauty fool you. This place can be as cold and ruthless as its ruler."

Another dragon snorted in my head. Issik. *"You didn't see me bitching about the heat. Suck it up, lava boy."*

A deep snarl rumbled up Zade's throat, bringing a smile to my lips. I missed the banter between them. Things had been so serious lately, that there wasn't much joshing going on between my dragons.

I had to agree with Zade, but I kept the thought to myself. No point in stirring up trouble. Of all the kingdoms, Iculon was the most daunting, and the task in front of me seemed equally as formidable. Then I got a glimpse of Issik's home.

Unlike the sharp angles of Crimson Keep, Issik's castle was all curves. Five domed towers made of arched windows circled upward, each one slightly taller than the one to its left. Their round roofs were shiny and smooth, scalloped like dragon scales. Thinner towers of glass jutted up to the clouds like shards of crystal. Hell, the entire multistory castle could have been constructed of glass for all I knew, and it was encased in a shimmering shield of blue magic—Issik's shield.

What would the castle's interior look like? Would the floors be made of ice, and the furniture of packed snow? I shuddered at the thought. The castle seemed so remote from everything, lonely even, I had seen only one small village on the other side of the lake, the smoke drifting up in stacks from the numerous chimneys. My gaze sought out Issik in the sky. It took a certain kind of prince to live in a castle such as this.

Balconies and staircases wrapped around the castle, going up and up. My awe made me momentarily forget the cold. I was grateful no trouble had befallen us during the journey. The last few days had taken a toll on my body.

"You're awfully quiet. It makes me wonder what is going on in that pretty head of yours," Zade pointed out, breaking me from my thoughts.

"I'm just drinking it all in. I can't believe we're going to be living here."

"The quicker you find the stone, the sooner we can get back to someplace warm."

I chuckled under my breath, a curl of warm air escaping my lips. "What if I like it here?" I challenged.

He snorted. *"You would be one of the very few who prefer Iculon over the other kingdoms. He might be handsome, but his sunny disposition keeps many from getting close."*

My braid slipped free of my hood, falling over my shoulder as Zade descended. Poor Issik. My heart grew heavy for him, for the loneliness in his life. I glanced at the castle of ice. If he asked me to live here with him, would I be able to withstand the cold, to be happy here?

I'd like to think I could.

Issik's castle was nestled in a valley surrounded by craggy mountains. Not the easiest place for dragons to land, but Zade and Issik both made it seem effortless. Zade landed on the uneven ground with a thud that shook the earth, kicking up snow under his clawed feet as they dug into the rock underneath.

Dragon shadows danced around us, and I noticed Jase and Kieran were still in the sky. "What's going on?" I asked, watching their dragon forms circle the castle and then take off in different directions. They had to be weary from the journey. I hadn't even done anything physical, and I was bone-tired.

"Border patrol. They'll do a sweep of the kingdom," Zade replied.

My gaze followed them until they were nothing but dark specks in the gray sky, before I slid off Zade, and turned to the castle. Issik and Zade shifted, leaving them both naked in the dead of winter. My cheeks burned, but I kept my eyes focused on them. They might be completely comfortable with their nakedness, but it still made me blush, even though I appreciated their physique.

Ahead, stood two glass doors that were easily twice as tall as the ones back on Earth. The glass was etched with a symbol as intricate as a snowflake. Iron framed the glass.

"If you don't open those doors, I'm going to freeze my balls off," Zade barked, his teeth chattering.

Issik glowered before slipping a hand under my elbow to help me make the slippery climb to the castle. "Maybe then you wouldn't be such a hothead."

The massive doors groaned open under Issik's command, and I got my first glimpse of the majestic frost castle. Inside, the halls were silent. The soles of my shoes clattering against the flagstone floor were the only sound. I found its emptiness strange for such a large estate. Where was the staff? I remembered Issik mentioning that his home was protected by a magical barrier. Was that the reason for the solitude?

The main hall was a glass dome with creamy white furnishings. A chandelier hung in the sitting room off to the left, its teardrop crystals sparkling from the firelight. The hearth was roaring and crackling, filling the room with toasty warmth. An oval velvet settee sat under the chandelier near the fire. White, carved stone framed all the doorways, and fur rugs overlaid the gray floors. No curtains covered the windows, letting in the glistening of the snow, ice, and mountains.

I lingered in the threshold, trying to picture Issik living there. From the paintings on the walls, to the tile floors, his home was nothing like I had imagined. No igloo vibes here. A half smile curved my lips at my silly assumptions.

A young woman, near my age, came flying around the corner then, a bundle of clothes clutched in her arms. The shuffling of her footsteps had preceded her, and I spun toward the sound, to find her skidding to a halt in front of me.

"Oh!" she gasped, gathering the clothing more securely as she gave me a look of wide-eyed curiosity. Her obsidian hair fell in waves down her back, while sincere admiration shone in her striking azure eyes. "You must be Olivia." She gave a slight bow with her head. "The kingdom has been buzzing about you for weeks. We've wondered when we'd get the chance to meet you."

The honor and respect she showed me were a first, her high regard for me made me nervous. I didn't want to mess up this first impression.

"I'm Juniper."

"It's a pleasure to meet you," I replied, hoping I'd find a friend in Juniper. Her demeanor and smile instantly made me feel relaxed and welcomed. I needed both at the moment.

Issik cleared his throat. "Now that the introductions are out of the way... Juniper?"

Twisting toward Issik and Zade, Juniper walked toward them, giving both a graceful bow and then handing them each a pile of clothes. She didn't bat an eye at the two naked dragons. "Where are lords Jase and Kieran?"

Lords? This was the first time I'd heard anyone give the descendants titles. I knew they were royalty here in the Veil—kings, actually, since their fathers were gone—but the title still sounded strange.

The Iculon castle seemed so formal, but not in a cold, uncaring way. Pride and joy were evident in Juniper's face, leading me to believe she was very happy here.

"They'll be here within the hour," Issik informed her. "You can leave their clothes here. I know they will be as grateful as I am."

"Everything is ready for your arrival," Juniper assured him.

"Thank you. I don't know what I'd do without you," he assured, slipping the pants over his hips. The dragons had no shame. How long would it take for me to be as comfortable with their nakedness?

Zade, now fully clothed, strutted into the sitting area, and poured himself a drink. The dark cherry liquid swirled in his cup as he brought it to his lips, sucking it dry in one gulp. "Hopefully, that will warm me up."

"How can you still be cold?" I asked, walking into the

room after him. Although the large fire added warmth, the overall temperature of the castle stayed at a pleasant coolness. Not the frigid, shivering kind.

Zade moved to stand in front of the roaring fire, a shudder rolling over the muscles of his back. "My blood isn't made for such a climate. Perhaps you should keep me warm, now that you share my power." A wicked gleam twinkled in his cinnamon eyes.

"How about I get you a fur coat instead?" Issik gruffly replied.

A giggle broke the silent glare between the Ice Prince and Hot Lips. I'd forgotten about Juniper. "Ignore them," I suggested, rolling my eyes. "I do."

She giggled again, and the sound echoed throughout the glass castle. I'd missed the sound of laughter in my life. Juniper gave me a bright smile. "We're going to be fast friends, Olivia. I just know it."

God knew I could use a friend.

After excusing herself, Juniper bound out of the room as lively as she had arrived, and Issik and I left Zade in front of the fire to tour the rest of his home.

"I thought the castle would be freezing. How is it so... tolerable?" I asked. In the Veil, there was no such thing as air conditioners or heaters. For all their finery and magic, they still lived without much of the technology we had on Earth.

"It's controlled with a spell."

Magic. I should have guessed.

"My father kept a healer on staff who also had other talents," he explained. His tone indicated there might have been more between his father and the healer. An affair possibly?

We walked up the stairs and down several drafty hallways. The craftsmanship in each kingdom never failed to impress me. Iculon was as opulent as the others, but in its own refined way.

"Juniper seems nice. Has she been here long?" I asked, longing to fill the quiet with chatter.

Issik thought about it for a moment. I could only imagine how the years blended together after so long. "Two years, I believe." His fingers forked through his silky blond hair. "Most of my staff has been with me for years. Juniper is the youngest in my care."

Was there anything between them? Something more than lord and subject? More than friends?

"Here are your rooms," Issik gestured, swinging open an ivory door. He leaned on the edge of the frame, waiting for me to pass through it.

"Rooms?" I echoed, lifting a brow.

My suite could have been an apartment in Chicago. When I first walked in, a sitting area with a small table for two greeted me. Through the next door was the sleeping chambers, having a joined bath and dressing room. The scent of lotus flowed from one room to the next, pure and sweet, and shimmering silver swirls adorned the soft blue walls.

"Does this room suit you?" Issik asked from his position by the doorway. He had been watching me as I explored.

Grinning, I spun to face him. "Are you kidding? I feel like a princess."

A smile played on his sensual lips—a rare treat from the Ice Prince. I wanted to make him smile every day of his life. "Good."

"It's so big. I don't know what to do with myself."

"It was my mother's."

I swallowed. "Are you sure it's okay that I stay here?"

He nodded. "She would be honored for you to take her rooms. You're royalty to me. I want you to be happy here."

My finger trailed over the ivory dresser, a hint of a smile on my lips as I looked at him. "How could anyone not be?"

Issik's icy blue eyes twinkled.

I only meant to lay down for a few minutes, the soft white bed was an invitation I couldn't resist. Yet, when I woke up, the sun was sinking low behind the mountains, immersing the room in hues of blues and pinks. The sunset was magnificent, and I was tempted to brave the snowy balcony.

My arms stretched upward as I sat up, while the low embers from the hearth in front of the bed toasted my toes. I padded over to the bathroom to wash my face, and unravel the braid from my hair—crimped locks cascaded over my shoulders in golden hues. I stared at my reflection, wrinkling my nose at the dusting of freckles that had darkened from my time in the Crimson sun, but the shadows that lurked under my eyes were fading. Turning my face to the right, the scar running along my cheek still shocked me. It was my face, but a roughness now marked more than just my skin.

I was different.

Swirling spots suddenly hurdled through my head, and I clutched the sides of the sink, hunched over with my eyes closed, and waiting for the black dots to cease. With slow, steady breaths, I inhaled and exhaled, riding out the dizzy spell until it passed.

What the hell was that?

Food. I needed to eat. It had been hours since breakfast.

Straightening, I stepped out of my quarters and set out to hunt down the descendants. I was a little surprised to find no one keeping guard at my door. They'd become relentless in their duty to protect me.

Speaking of protecting…

My fingers dug into my pocket, fumbling for the stone. I relaxed at the feel of the smooth surface against my fingertips. Perhaps it wasn't the smartest idea to carry it around with me. I needed to find a secure place for it in my rooms.

Either I was getting acquainted with castle life, or the circular layout of Issik's home made it easier for me to find my way around the palace. Effortlessly, I hung a left at the bottom of the staircase, and went toward the deep voices emanating from down the hall. My steps halted alongside an ivory pillar, needing to steady myself as another wave of lightheadedness shot through me.

Damn this dizziness.

However, it lasted no more than a few seconds. The scent of something savory wafting in the air made my stomach rumble, and I stepped away from the pillar to find Issik and the others lounged at the table in the dining room. Jase and Kieran had already returned from their patrol of the grounds, but the room went silent at my approach.

I paused at the empty seat, my hands resting on the high back of the chair. "What is it?"

Suddenly, their food became very interesting, and no one met my gaze. Something had happened.

Kieran shifted in his seat. "Jase and I ran into a small problem during our patrol."

My gaze bounced between the two, expectantly. "What kind of problem?" I finally prodded, seeing as they weren't voluntarily offering the information.

Jase lifted the crystal decanter of red wine, and poured himself a generous portion. "The portal. It's weakening, leaving the Veil exposed for other creatures to slip in." His voice remained calm while he spoke. "Kieran and I found a pair of dusanac roaming the western border."

A chill scurried down my spine. "Oh," I replied, sliding into the seat. "Do I want to know what those are?"

"No," was the uniform reply from everyone at the table.

I scrunched my nose while Issik poured me a glass of wine.

"It's nothing Jase and I couldn't handle," Kieran added, noticing my face had lost a shade of color.

This time. But what about the next time? Or the one after that? It made me nervous when they went out to fight. They might have been born warriors and bestowed magical gifts, but under the circumstances, I couldn't help but worry.

Until the curse was broken, and their strength was restored, they were vulnerable.

A bowl of thick, creamy soup and a basket of bread was placed in front of me. My lips curved into a smile of thanks to the older woman while I picked up my spoon.

The first taste of soup was blissful, and it was an effort to keep from sighing. Ripping off a hunk of bread, I dunked it into the steaming bowl, letting it soak in the broth. The bowl was empty in minutes, and it wasn't until my spoon scraped the bottom that I became aware the descendants were watching me.

"You look... better," Zade offered, his chin propped against his closed hand.

"I'm going to take that as a compliment."

"I only meant that a bit of rest did you good," he mumbled, stuffing bread into his mouth.

If that was the case, then why did I still feel so tired? My body felt off-centered, like my equilibrium had quit on me.

"Have you had any inclinations on where to find the Star of Frost?" Issik asked, leaning forward.

Focusing on my plate, I shook my head. "Not yet." How did I tell him everything about me felt wrong? I would figure it out. My body probably just needed more sleep, a chance to decompress. In a few days, I'd be as good as new.

"We'll begin our search tomorrow, if you're feeling up to it," Jase informed, his food forgotten.

I swallowed, forcing my face to stay neutral and not hide the anxiety I felt. Mentally, I was more than ready to see this curse end. I just hoped my body and the stones cooperated. "I'm ready," I assured him with a soft smile. "What about the creatures Tianna is summoning through the portal?" I asked, nibbling on the last roll of bread.

Kieran swirled his wine before taking a sip. "You don't need to worry about that. We'll take care of them. It is our responsibility as the leaders of the Veil to keep our kingdoms safe, but when venturing out, we'll need to take precautions. Lucky for us, the conditions in Iculon don't make it a desirable place to seek shelter."

With that settled, silence fell over the room. We were all thinking about the future and what it held. My mind kept going back to the portal, and the untold dangers we might come up against. I wasn't fond of things trying to kill me.

Of all the other kingdoms, and the people who lived there, Iculon had the smallest population. Was leaving the other lands unattended wise? Of course, the descendants would monitor their lands, but it wasn't the same as them presiding over their kingdoms daily.

We lingered at the dinner table for a few hours, drinking and the dragons reminiscing about old times—times before the Great War and how different the Veil had been. Seeing the descendants relaxed from the wine, and the pleasant conversation was a nice change. They needed this, a few hours without responsibility, without the war looming over their heads, and without constantly thinking about being cursed.

I was careful this time to not overindulge in spirits. My head felt fogged enough without being drunk. The meal had done very little to still the spinning in my head. Although my body yelled at me to lie down, I couldn't make myself leave. Being with them like this—free of inhibitions—was something I wanted to treasure. I imagined this was how they were before being cursed by the witch.

Fun. Playful. Wild. Yet still, royalty—powerful and commanding.

Every so often Issik would glance at me, worry

creasing his forehead. The emotional bond between us made him perceptive to what I was feeling. "Kieran, will you escort Olivia to her room? It's late. We could all use some sleep."

My eyes met Issik's, and I gave him a stern look, calling him out on his subtle command for me to go to bed.

He bowed his head slightly at me, as if saying, "You're welcome."

What was I to do with these meddling dragons, always thinking they knew what was best for me?

Sighing, I conceded that going to bed was wise. The chair scooted across the cool tiled floor as I stood, but then the room gave a horrendous lurch, and I stumbled. The smell of the woods after a rainfall surrounded me as I fell into strong arms.

"Hey, there," Kieran murmured near my ear, his hands steadying me. "How many glasses of wine did you have?"

"One," I mumbled, trying to make my eyes focus on his dark green tunic.

"Hmm." His lips pursed in an amused half smirk. "If you say so."

He lowered a shoulder, and I backed up a step, anticipating the maneuver they were so fond of using on me. "I can walk," I stated.

Kieran winked. "Where's the fun in that?" Still, he didn't try to lift me into his arms again, letting me lumber my way to the base of the stairs.

My hand gripped the banister for balance as I kicked off my satin slippers. A sigh left my lips. "I've been dying to take my shoes off," I explained at Kieran's lifted brows.

A wicked grin spread over his lips. "You're not required to wear them."

"Now you tell me," I muttered, bending down to pick up my discarded shoes. My bare feet were silent on the stairs, and I kept a hand running up the smooth banister. Such a sophisticated home for a brooding dragon. "Did you know Issik's family?" I asked, curious about who they had been, particularly the woman who had chosen to spend her life in a frozen tundra. She must have loved Issik's father very much.

Kieran strolled beside me, keeping close as if he sensed something was off with me. "Not well. Our fathers would summon the council of the five kingdoms twice a year, to discuss the state of the Veil. At around age five, I was instructed to attend the meetings with my father as the heir of Viperus. It was at these conferences that I met the other descendants. Although we were required to listen in on discussions, the five of us often found ourselves getting into trouble."

They had once told me that prior to the curse they hadn't been friends. "What were your parents like?" I inquired, hoping it wasn't too painful of a question.

"Normal, I guess."

"I find that hard to believe."

His full lips curved upward. "If you take out the dragon aspect, my life growing up was average. My mother made sure I had balance between being the prince to a kingdom and just being a boy. I spent most of my childhood playing and running around with the staff's children, terrorizing my tutors, and exploring the woods surrounding my home. They never treated me as a pampered prince. I had classes, the same as everyone else, but between those, I was given extra studies regarding the kingdoms and my position as the dragon heir for Viperus. My mother was loving and kind. She had an affinity for plants. They thrived under her attention."

What a perfect match for a king whose home was nestled deep in the woods. "Did you have any siblings?" Not once had any of the descendants mentioned brothers or sisters. I was an only child myself. Had they wished for a younger sibling to play with as I had?

"Like the other descendants, we all grew up as only children. It's part of the dragon gene. Only one heir is ever born to a dragon."

"Are they always male?" The folds of my dress swished in black waves as I climbed.

Kieran's hand quickly slipped under my arm, catching me as I tripped on the hem of my skirt. "It is rare for a dragon to have a girl, but not impossible. Jase's grandmother carried the dragon line in his family."

His grandmother had been a dragon. I was utterly fascinated by the family history of the descendants. "I wish I could have seen the Veil before the Great War."

The grin on his face was infectious. "You would have loved it."

"I already do." I wanted to tell him that I'd seen his mother, that she was beautiful and had helped me, but I stayed silent.

He leaned in, pressing a kiss to my lips, and the light-headedness returned.

It's just the kiss, I told myself. *Kieran's kisses always leave me dizzy.*

True, but this? This was different.

"Olivia?" he murmured.

41

"Hmm," I replied, my voice sounding as if it was a million miles away from my body.

The pad of his thumb brushed over my cheek. "Are you feeling okay?"

"I-I'm not sure. My head..." The shoes fell from my grip as I lifted my hands to my temples—the whirling wouldn't quit. Suddenly, the stairs tilted and spun.

A cool hand pressed to my forehead. "You're burning up."

I was? Strange. I didn't feel hot.

The ground was swept out from under me, and I didn't protest his offer to carry me this time. "You need to be in bed," he informed in a disapproving tone, that was out of character for the rebellious poison dragon.

"I need to find the last star," I mumbled, even as my head fell onto his shoulder.

Kieran snorted. "Not tonight you don't."

"You smell good."

A low chuckle rumbled against my body, and the sound followed me into the darkness that swallowed me whole.

In the distance, the shuffling of feet and grumbling of deep voices crossed over the canyon in my mind. The grumblings intensified, disturbing my sleep. Why was I so tired? And why was it so hard to wake up?

It took considerable effort, but I peeled open my eyes and found all four descendants in my room. Two were sleeping in chairs, while another paced at the foot of the bed, and the fourth stared intently into the low-burning hearth.

What was going on?

Why were they all in my room?

Had I been hurt?

I wiggled in the bed, testing out my limbs. Everything seemed to be in working order, so I sat up and cleared my throat, finding it scratchy and dry. Water. I needed water.

"Olivia?" Issik breathed. He was the dragon pacing over the snow white rug on my bedroom floor. At the sight of me stirring, he halted dead in his tracks. His eyes flew to my face, and the next moment he was at my side, pressing a hand to my forehead. The others jumped up and surrounded my bed like a flock of mother hens.

"How are you feeling?" Kieran anxiously asked.

Ten seconds ago, I would have said fine, but the sudden movement of sitting up had thrown my stomach for a loop. "I'm going to throw up," I rasped.

The descendants backed up in unison.

Before I could further embarrass myself, I rolled out of bed and stumbled into the bathroom to hurl what little was in my stomach into the sink, but once I was finished, the nausea disappeared. I washed my face with cold water, rinsed out my mouth, and was pleased to see my skin had a tad of color to it.

What was going on with me? Had I eaten something bad last night? It couldn't have possibly been the wine. A single glass wouldn't have given me a hangover like this one.

Trembling steps took me back to the room, and climbed onto the middle of the bed. Folding my legs, I searched their gazes. "What happened?" My voice sounded odd in my head—stuffy, like my ears were filled with cotton balls.

"You collapsed and have had a fever for two days," Kieran replied first from his reclined spot in the chair. His black pants and tunic were wrinkled, as if he'd been in the same spot for hours.

Two days! What? How the hell had two days gone by? "I've been asleep the whole time?"

"In and out. We were beginning to worry," Jase confessed from the foot of the bed, where he stood frowning at me.

I'd lost two days that could have been spent looking for the star. "What caused me to get so sick?" It hadn't been like any illness I'd ever had before, definitely not the flu or a cold. But what was it?

Issik leaned a shoulder against one of the four posts at the corners of the bed. His eyes moved over my face, searching for something. "We don't know," he finally answered.

Jase's brow arched, the scowl lifting from his face. "We were hoping you could tell us."

"Me?" I forked a hand through my disheveled hair, wracking my brain for my last memories. "I remember being dizzy most of the day, but didn't think much of it. Kieran and I were walking up the stairs and..." I hit a black wall—slammed into it, to be more accurate. I pounded on the mental block in my memory, but it wouldn't budge; it wouldn't crack.

"You fainted," Kieran supplied, seeing the struggle and confusion on my face.

"On the stairs?" It was the last place I remembered. "And I didn't break my neck?"

Kieran put a hand to his heart, looking wounded. "I'm insulted. You were in my arms. Do you not remember me carrying you? Furthermore, do you honestly believe I would let you fall?"

"No, of course not. Given my history, it isn't unreasonable to expect that accidents will occur around me. I'm not used to having someone around to catch me. Thank you."

His emerald eyes sparkled. "Always. It was my pleasure."

Zade snorted from the other side of the bed, the deep red of his shirt bringing out the flecks of gold in his eyes. "You'd take any excuse to get her into your arms."

"And you wouldn't?" Kieran challenged.

Slowly, my fingertips massaged my temples, and I considered fainting again just to put an end to their banter before things got out of hand. A cup of tea appeared in front of me.

"Drink this," Issik commanded.

Eager to soothe my dry throat, I obeyed. The tea was sweetened with honey and something fruity like passion-fruit. I sipped half of the cup in silence, and the sudden quiet had me studying them. They were acting weird.

Something was wrong, but what?

Lowering the cup of tea to my lap, I shot the four of them a look, daring them to avert their gazes. "What aren't you telling me?"

Zade shifted on his feet, and Kieran's eyes darted to the rumpled bed around me, avoiding my questioning glare. Jase rubbed at the back of his neck, the chest muscles under his white tunic tensing.

A rumble of irritation sounded at the back of my throat. "Someone better explain."

Jase huffed. "You are the most troublesome female."

My arms crossed over my chest. "And whose fault is that?"

Kieran's lips twitched.

"You were glowing while you slept," Issik murmured, waiting for my reaction.

I blinked. "What did you say?"

"We'd never seen anything like it," Jase admitted, but he didn't sound happy about it. In fact, his lips were turned down again. "Your skin was emitting a white glow, like you were bathed in starlight."

If I hadn't been in shock, I might have found the idea of glowing fascinating, but given the numerous unusual events in my life recently, this was probably not a good thing. "Am I dying?"

"Doubtful. If you were going to die because of this, you'd already be dead," Zade assured.

Issik's hand thumped the back of Zade's head. "Smooth."

"What the idiot is trying to say," Jase began, "is we believe the illness might have been caused by the exorbitant amount of changes your body has gone through over the last few months. These past few days in particular."

They had expressed their concerns before about this, and it appeared those concerns had finally caught up with me. "What am I supposed to do about it? We can't afford for me to spend days in bed."

Jase sat on the edge of the mattress. "Well, for starters, the next time you start to feel unwell, you tell us. Other than that, I'm not sure we can do more than hope your body has stabilized after resting these last few days."

My fingers tapped the side of my teacup. "I swear that even if my pinky tingles, I will let you know."

Snickers followed, and as hard as Jase tried to keep a straight face, his lush lips gave out into a smile. Leaning in, he brushed those lips over my cheek. "How many times are you going to stop my heart?" he whispered.

"Today?"

He shook his head at me.

I placed the teacup on the nightstand and stretched, realizing for the first time I was in my nightshirt. Someone had changed my clothes. My gut clenched. Which one had it been? *Get it together. It's not like they haven't seen you naked before, and it doesn't matter who.* They had cared enough to watch over me and keep me comfortable. All of them. Softening the tightening of my lips, I lifted my eyes.

"Did anything happen while I was… indisposed?" Like had they found any information on the Star of Frost? Had Tianna made any threats while I'd been dozing? Did any other creatures slip through the portal? So many gloomy possibilities.

Kieran crossed his long legs at his ankles, his features relaxed. "It was as quiet as a mouse around here, other than your snoring."

"I do not snore," I protested as I flung one of the pillows on the bed across the room at him. He laughed as he caught the pillow missile, using his dragon reflexes.

"So, I guess I shouldn't mention the drool?"

"Not if you don't want me to set fire to that pillow on your lap," I warned him. It was an empty threat.

He lifted a single brow. "You can do that?"

Suddenly, the feathered pillow resting on Kieran erupted into flames, and I squeaked at the sight of the blaze engulfing the silk like it had been doused in gasoline. He jumped out of his chair with ninja-like agility, tossing the fiery pillow to the tiled floor close to my bed.

48

As I scrambled backward—oblivious because of how close to the mattress it fell—Issik reacted, moving around the bed with inhuman speed. He put the flames out with a burst of ice. The lovely white fabric was now charred with black soot, and frayed. And just at that moment, I teetered toward the ground.

Zade caught me, depositing me back onto the safety of the mattress as four dragons scowled down at me. In less than a minute, the room had erupted into chaos, all caused by me. This had to be a record.

Shit. I hadn't meant for that to happen. It was only a fleeting thought, and yet...

The pungent scent of burnt fabric filled the room, while Kieran waved off the plume of smoke. Issik's ice blue, dragon eyes stared at me with a mixture of bewilderment and exasperation.

"Sorry," I mumbled with a sheepish look, tempted to pull the covers over my head. "I didn't mean for it to catch fire. I never would—" Emotion clogged my throat. What had I done? What was happening to me? I would never intentionally hurt Kieran, but I hadn't been able to stop the power from releasing. It had been a simple thought and whoosh, the pillow had gone up in flames.

"Hey, Blondie," Kieran murmured. His finger hooked under my chin, tipping my face to meet his. "You have nothing to apologize for."

I wasn't surprised he didn't hold me responsible, none of them would, but it still didn't change the fact that I was unpredictable, and potentially dangerous. A time would come when I had to deal with the changes happening to me, and that time was sooner rather than later. None of us could afford for me to become a loose cannon, especially when we were so close to ending this curse.

"Zade, any thoughts on how to control this?" Jase pressed.

I knew they didn't mean to make me feel like an experiment, but I couldn't help but feel as if I was on display, a puzzle they had to solve.

"None of us have that kind of magic," Zade replied, his hand scratching at his chin as he continued to stare at me.

Kieran's eyes looked me up and down. "I'm not sure any of us have the skills to teach her how to wield magic. She seems to be able to manipulate our powers in ways we can't."

My gaze fell, and I analyzed the quilt as though it were the most interesting thing.

"I'm curious now about what she can do with our other abilities," Jase added.

I rolled my eyes and dropped down onto the bed, groaning.

A soft knock sounded on the door, and Juniper poked in her head. I was sitting at the table in my sitting room, and I waved her forward, glad to see a friendly face. She carried a tray with broth and crackers that she laid on the far corner of the table.

"I'm glad to see you're awake. They've been going mad with worry and driving everyone crazy."

"I should probably apologize then," I mumbled, distracted by the food.

She chuckled. "Are you hungry?"

"Starving," I admitted, giving her a grateful smile. "Thank you, Juniper, for the food." My stomach growled at the aroma of the savory broth, and my mouth watered. "It smells delicious."

"Our cook is the best in the Veil. This is her special brew that is guaranteed to cure all ailments."

Juniper wore a simple teal dress that came to her calves. The sleeves were a short bell cut over her slender shoulders. She might choose to live in the coldest region of the Veil, but she looked like she had stepped straight out of summer. Which reminded me, it was springtime, regardless of the snow and ice surrounding the castle, and summer was around the corner. Suppressing a sigh, I picked up the spoon on the tray next to the bowl of broth.

Juniper smoothed the folds of her dress. "The entire castle has been worrying about you. We're glad to see you're up and about." So the staff knew I'd been sick. What did they think of me? I was supposed to be some savior, and yet, I'd been knocked out cold for two days.

"Will you stay with me? I don't like to eat alone." The descendants were either busy taking care of kingdom duties, or snoring in my bed—like my current assigned babysitter, Zade. I didn't blame him for being exhausted and had left him undisturbed in my sleeping chambers.

She glanced over her shoulder at the door, then at the empty chair in front of me. For a brief moment, I thought she might refuse. "I have a few minutes before anyone notices I'm gone." The iron legs of the chair scraped lightly over the floor as she sat with a poise I'd never possess.

My shoulders straightened a fraction, as I tried to match her posture without looking like a fool. Juniper was bred to live in castles and stand beside dragon kings. Me? I didn't know how I fit into this world. The Veil was my home; I didn't question that anymore. This was where I wanted to be—with the descendants. But what happened after? After the curse was broken? After Tianna was dead? After we saved the world?

I sipped on the spoonful of hot broth, testing my stomach's ability to keep down food. It was divine, and my greedy appetite wanted to gulp it down all at once, but I forced myself to go slow, savoring the flavors of chicken stock and herbs with hints of onion. "Do you like living in Iculon?" I asked, blowing on the spoon.

She shrugged. "I like the quiet and the solitude. The other castles already had full staffs, and although we're always given a choice, I wanted a simple life without drama."

"It doesn't get lonely?" I was genuinely curious about her life here. It was so different than the other kingdoms, so remote and harsh, and yet this girl was sweet and lively in a refreshing way.

"Not usually. There is so much to do to keep up a castle, particularly since Issik keeps a smaller staff than the others." She played with the charm hanging around her neck, a pretty little medallion. And as she gnawed on her lip, I could tell she had more to say but wasn't sure if it was her place.

I offered her an encouraging smile. "I'm glad you're here."

She smiled in return. "You're not like I pictured. He's different with you, you know? We all noticed the changes in him, over the last few months since you arrived."

"How so?" I prodded, eating another spoonful of soup. She had piqued my interest.

"Warmer, if that's possible."

Dabbing at the corners of my mouth with a napkin, I leaned back in my chair. "Warm is not a word I'd normally use to describe the Ice Prince."

She lifted her brows at the nickname I'd given Issik. "You care about him."

I nodded. "I care about all of them."

The approval on her face reached her eyes. "We might have only just met, but I can't help but hope once the curse is broken, you choose Issik and come to live here. Call me a hopeless romantic, but you bring out the best in him. He needs someone like you to thaw that frozen heart. He's in love with you. And it would be great to have a friend close to my age," she added in earnest.

My belly fluttered. It hit me in the heart knowing that other people could see what I felt, but as full as my heart was with the descendants, a part of me was afraid. What would happen after the curse was lifted? Would I be forced to choose between them? Would they still care for me as they did now? And the big question that haunted my future: Would they marry? They were royalty, the last dragons, and were required to continue their lineage. I understood their responsibilities. I just didn't know how I would fit into their lives, and that hurt. Unexpected tears stung my eyes as I lowered my lashes, stirring the broth in aimless circles.

"I didn't mean to upset you," Juniper said quietly, having noticed the gleam in my eyes before I could avert my gaze. "I'm sorry. I should get back—"

My hand laid over Juniper's, stopping her from

jumping up from the table and bolting, before I got the chance to explain my sudden shift in emotions. "You didn't," I assured her, lifting my glossy eyes to meet hers. "I'm being silly." I brushed the tears away before they could fall. "It's been an insane few months, and I never expected to fall in love. I don't know what to do about these feelings," I attempted to explain, unsure if she knew what I meant.

She observed me as I collected myself. "You're in love with all of them, aren't you?" Intrigue glistened in her expression.

"Is it that obvious?"

"If someone pays enough attention, but I don't think you need to worry about gossip. Most of the people in the Veil would be glad to see the four dragon heirs happy and smiling. Other than a few glimpses from time to time, they haven't been truly happy since the day the curse befell them. It would be a welcomed change. But that's not to say the others wouldn't be jealous. Many have tried to claim the heart of a dragon, but until now, none have succeeded."

"You don't find it strange?"

"It's not for me to judge. If there is one thing I've learned, is that nothing is impossible. Who knows? This might be exactly what fate planned."

I chewed on her words, unsure if I believed in fate. I wanted to believe we carved out our own destiny. "I never imagined I'd feel so strongly about four different men. I'm unsure how to handle our relationship, to find a balance between the five of us." My body also was attempting to find balance amidst the powers I now held. Perhaps they were linked? Or perhaps I was reading too much into the connection between the power of the stones and the dragons. Was that the reason I had such intense feelings for the four descendants? Because I'd been chosen?

Could it be destiny after all?

"I'd say your instincts have been leading you, and it's worked so far. Don't overthink it. Let what feels right guide you. They are as puzzled by you as you are by your feelings," she offered with more wisdom than her youth suggested.

I chuckled. "Keeping the descendants on their toes is my full-time job. I knew I'd like you."

Juniper had been right about many things, including the healing properties of the broth. I was feeling more stable and almost myself again.

Almost.

We set out on foot, the snow crunching under my boots as we walked. It was so densely packed in some places, that the descendants took turns lifting me over patches to keep from falling behind. Rogue flakes of snow sputtered from the overcast sky, and the winds howled like a lone wolf looking for its pack.

It had taken some convincing to get the dragons to venture out of the castle with me, but after two additional days of being fussed over, I needed fresh air and purpose. I must have said the words "I'm fine" at least a hundred times, but still, they wouldn't let me lift a finger. It wasn't until I threatened to go out on my own that they begrudgingly agreed.

However, as soon as we were about to leave, Kieran had dragged his feet, being a total diva, and stalling our departure in the hopes I would change my mind. Then, they each had come up with something they had to attend to before we left. After Issik announced he had some papers that had to be signed, I put my foot down, warning him that those damn papers that were suddenly so important were about to go up in flames.

And because they all knew how temperamental my abilities were, we had left the castle promptly.

Tugging the deep purple cloak closer around me, I tipped my head down into the hood to escape the bristling winds. Why the hell were we traipsing around on foot? I much preferred to travel by dragonback. Jase wanted to keep close to the castle for our first journey out, with the portals only partially shielded by the curse, he didn't want to take any chances of running into something nasty.

I didn't doubt Tianna had her eyes on us. In fact, I swore I could feel them staring at us from the shimmering surface of the Pool of Mirrors.

Bitch. The word seethed in my mind, fueled by every cut, every drop of blood spilled, and every person she'd hurt.

"Who do I need to kill?" Zade asked beside me. His proximity chased away some of the cold. It was handy to have him around in the frozen tundra.

Then I remembered. I had fire of my own. There was no reason for me to freeze to death, assuming I didn't accidentally set myself ablaze. It might not have been the best time to test out my magic, but the urge to let the tingle of fire spread in my veins was strong.

My teeth ground together. "The usual. A witch with the ugliest shade of red hair." That was a lie.

In truth, her hair was like autumn at midnight—a beautiful wine color that tumbled down her back in lush waves. She didn't deserve hair so stunning, and considering how old the hag was, it was obvious she was completely fake. Spelled, from her flawless skin to her perfect boobs. Knowing that she used magic to keep her looks and her youth, made her vain—a weakness worth exploiting if the opportunity ever presented itself. I had once seen her without the glamour. Once was enough. "Hag" wasn't a strong enough word to describe what I had seen in the mirror's reflection.

I shuddered.

"Her time will come," Zade promised.

"Whose time?" Kieran asked, bounding through the snow to catch up to Zade and me. The glimmer in his emerald eyes reminded me of a kid tromping through the first snowfall of the year.

"Never mind. Just keep your eyes open."

Kieran lifted a hand, shielding his squinting eyes from the glare of the sun. "It's hard to see with all this snow reflecting the light."

"You learn to adjust," Issik grumbled, having no problems at all as he moved. The man was born to maneuver through this land effortlessly, while the rest of us struggled.

"I'd rather not," Kieran mumbled.

This was going to be my day—a constant soundtrack of bickering dragons. It might have driven a normal person crazy, but I found some comfort in the banter—a familiarity and unity. They were like family in the way they interacted. I was part of something. I belonged.

"You figure out how to track these things yet, Blondie?"

I shot Kieran a sideways glance. "It helps if you stand on your head, and spin three times in a circle. It gets the energy flowing."

A snicker escaped Zade, while Jase rubbed his hands together to warm them. "So, you haven't felt anything since coming to the castle?"

Sighing, I refrained from pointing out that half of my time there had been spent unconscious. "No." My fingers stroked the star inside the lined pocket of my cloak. Now would be a great time for those stars to give me some kind of hint.

Nothing.

We walked for over two hours, never wandering too far from the castle. Every part of me was stiff, aching, and frozen to the bone. Turned out even my powers had limitations. The fire in my veins had died out an hour ago, draining me to the point where I was tempted to just plop down in the snow and rest. Five minutes was all I needed. My body pleaded with me to stop as my feet dragged on over the harsh terrain.

Not a whisper or a tingle of the star had spoken to me.

Beyond the foothills gleamed the crystal castle, and I kept the sparkling glass walls in my sight as motivation for my feet to keep moving. One foot in front of the other. The tip of my nose was red, and my cheeks stung from the blistering cold.

We had avoided the bordering evergreens on the north and west sides of the castle. The woods were dense, and flecks of snow stuck to the needled branches. Issik's gaze kept shifting toward the snow-veiled woods. A deep glower came onto his face.

"We need to get back to the castle," he announced after yet another glance at the trees. "Something's coming."

A growl split the air and got carried by the wind, making it sound as if it went on for miles. We all came to a sudden halt. "Shit," Jase hissed, taking a stance in front of me. The muscles on his back rippled through his heavy black cloak.

"Is the devourer still out here?" I asked quietly. The devourer was a shadowy monster I'd rather not meet again.

"Yes," Jase said in a clipped tone.

Pulling the flaps of my cloak further around me, I moved to stand closer to Zade for both protection and warmth. "Do they growl?" I asked.

Zade slipped an arm around my waist, tugging me into his arms. His cinnamon eyes weren't looking at me, but in the direction the growl had been heard. To my great dismay, a series of cries called out, one after the other, as if the beasts were talking to each other. Whatever was coming, wasn't alone. "No. That was something else," Zade answered.

"Fun," I replied, heavy on the sarcasm.

Jase turned so he and I were back to back. Whether it was a conscious decision or not, the descendants moved to surround me from all angles. The earth went silent as the five of us listened, and scanned the surrounding evergreens piled in snow. Something was hunting us.

I didn't have the enhanced hearing they did, so I relied on the language of their bodies to warn me. Their muscles hardened; their eyes glowed; and scales papered their arms and neck as they called their dragons to the surface without fully completing the shift.

"We should go now," Issik suggested. His fingers had

elongated into razor-sharp claws, and although his mouth was saying one thing, his body was poised for a fight.

The winter breeze stirred Kieran's spiky green hair. "It's too late. They're here."

Six shadowy figures emerged from the towering pines, with eyes so black they appeared to be made from the depths of the underworld. Covered in thick fur, the creatures stood on four legs. Sharp claws curled from their massive paws, digging deep into the snow for traction. They had the appearance of wolves, but on a much larger scale. Beside their erect ears, polished horns curled like talons.

They were creatures of nightmares told to little children to scare them into obedience. Their eyes haunted me the most, filled with a greedy bloodlust that chilled my soul. I had a hunch these creatures killed for sport. Tianna wouldn't need to spell them to do her bidding. These animals would tear apart anything that crossed their path.

Including us.

"What are they?" I whispered, not that putting a name to the creatures would make killing them any easier. There really should be a handbook of mythical creatures.

"Direhound," Issik hissed, his fingers flexing the claws that extended in place of his human nails.

"Are they... friendly?" I gulped, distributing my weight evenly on both feet in the snow. I knew it was a dumb question, but at some point, our bad luck had to run out. Right?

Not today it appeared.

The pack of predators paused at the edge of the clearing, eyeing us, their white teeth bared in greeting.

Removing his hand from the small of my back, Zade cracked his neck. "Does that answer your question?"

Loud and clear. "Okay, guys. What's the plan?"

Several glares fell on me, but I ignored them. I'd proved I could fight alongside these warriors... sort of. "Don't die," Jase instructed me, removing a dagger from inside his boot. "And don't do anything stupid."

My fingers curled around the smooth ebony hilt of the weapon Jase offered to me. "I like it. Simple."

"Now might be a good time to try out those new skills, Blondie." Kieran grinned, flashing a pair of dragon canines that had lengthened in his mouth. These partial shifts weren't something I was used to—a blend of human and dragon. Did it take more or less of their strength?

I'd have to worry about that later.

As if a signal had been given, the six direhounds surged forward, paws flying over the snow and icy ground with an ease that made me groan. Issik drew back a clawed hand and sliced it across one of the direhound's throats as it lunged for him. Blood sprayed the pure white ground, but the beast clamped on to Issik's arm, taking him down with it.

A scream lodged in my throat, but I had my own problems.

Kieran and Zade were each engaged with a direhound of their own, leaving Jase and me still back to back while three direhounds circled us, their teeth gleaming with their snarls. I wanted to run—the muscles in my body imploring me to get as far away as possible—but I clamped my jaw tight.

I was done running.

Screw this.

Screw the witch.

I stared at the direhound in front of me. Its soulless eyes were like a portal into the pits of hell. The animal's breath came out of its nostrils in short pants. Up close, its size was intimidating—as large as a bear. One swipe with a paw and I'd be out cold. Terror gripped me.

If I was going to learn to fight, to truly defend myself, then I needed to stop thinking I was helpless and feeling like a frightened kitten. "You want me. Come get me," I taunted it, keeping my voice low.

"Olivia," Jase hissed. "Are you trying to get yourself killed?" His back flexed against mine, while he kept his eyes zeroed in on the direhounds in front of him.

"I'm doing what Kieran suggested. Testing my powers."

"I didn't realize that included taunting them," Jase snapped.

"I'm multitasking."

The direhounds were growing impatient, the thirst for the kill growing in their eyes. From either side of us, the sounds of flesh tearing, bones crunching, and teeth gnashing filled the air, but I couldn't look to see how the others were faring.

"Brace yourself," Jase hissed through his teeth. "They're about to—"

In a uniform attack, the three beasts rushed forward—one at me and the other two went for Jase. The hound was only a few feet from me when it leaped. Its giant paws unfurled in the air. Bewildered, all I could do was stare, waiting for contact.

Whoosh.

I landed on my back with a jarring impact, my head hitting the snow with a dizzying thud. Hot metallic blood pooled on my tongue, and I swallowed it as I scrambled to get up, but the beast was quick, a whiff of my fear filling its nostrils. Its front paw smashed down on my shoulder, pinning me in the compacted snow. Saliva dripped from its canines onto my face, and I grimaced, the slime falling down my cheek slow and thick, like a slug.

The direhound's head leaned forward so that its cold, wet nose touched mine, panting its foul breath over my face. Death stared down at me from those black pupils. Was this how I met my end? Killed by a furry beast on steroids?

I wanted to give up, to just let go. My body felt so cold and tired, and the creature was so strong. Hadn't I already been through enough? A dark void seemed to come over me, feeding and fueling a seed of doubt until it spread like wildfire.

"Olivia!" one of the descendants bellowed.

That dark, pitiful place I'd been sucked into vanished on a phantom wind, and I remembered who I was, what my purpose was, and what I could do. Venomous power coursed through my body, sharp and cool. My palms surged forward, clasping the direhound's chest as my nails dug in, past the thick fur and the undercoat to flesh. The beast snarled in warning at the piercing of my nails.

"Suck on this, asshole." I released the toxin that had been gathering inside me. Poison seeped from my fingers and into the animal whose eyes went wide at the first trickle of venom, but I held on, even when it jerked its head.

The beast let out a scream that was eerily human, and I knew the poison was doing its job. My ears rang as the creature took its last wheezing breath, collapsing on top of me. I didn't have time to recover. Using both my feet and hands, I pushed at the carcass of the direhound, rolling it off me.

Shoving to my feet, I took in the scene before me. The white ground was soaked with blood and grotesque body parts I didn't wish to identify—I didn't want to risk losing the contents of my stomach.

"Jase!" Issik's roaring warning made my head whip around as I sought out each descendant.

Two of the direhounds had the tranquility dragon pinned to the ground. They had been smart enough to avoid Jase's dragon breath by holding the side of Jase's face to the snow with a paw. Angry scratches ran down his neck and had torn through the side of his shirt, blood soaking the material. Those stormy violet eyes connected with mine, silently commanding me to run, to save myself.

I didn't think, only reacted. Something about seeing the beasts on top of Jase, snapping its fangs and growling in his face, severed the thread on my control. Molten fire burned through my veins, the switch between powers as simple as blinking. Poison gave way to fire. Rage or a wild instinct to protect what was mine burst out of me.

Sensing my approach, the direhound sunk its teeth into the fleshy part of Jase's shoulder. It dug in deep, blood oozing out of the side of the mutt's muzzle and dripping down Jase's arm. My gut twisted in a white-hot rage that cut through my senses.

Ropes of fire unleashed from both my hands, one end wrapping around my wrists, the other snapping free toward the direhounds. Fire hissed as it connected with one of the beasts' back, dissolving a patch of fur. I smacked the other in the muzzle, and a shriek of pain pierced the air.

Nostrils flaring, the beasts faced me, identifying me as their biggest threat. I didn't hesitate when I pulled the whips of flames back toward me. Sensing my intent, the duo charged, their paws pounding into the ground. Someone might have screamed my name, but I couldn't hear anything past the roaring in my own head.

My cloak splayed out around me, the wind picking up the ends of the velvet material. Flicking my wrists with a calculated precision I didn't know I possessed, the ropes of fire wrapped around the direhounds' throats, and with one quick yank, I snapped their necks. The crunching of bones was music to my ears. Satisfaction like I'd never felt before coursed alongside the power swimming in my veins. They were companions, one feeding off the other.

It scared the shit out of me.

I liked the power, the feeling of being feared. What did that say about me? About who I was becoming?

The fire inside me fizzled out, the flaming ropes and my energy dissipating with it, and I sunk to my knees in the snow.

"Holy shit," Zade breathed. "Did you see that?"

"Olivia's a badass." Kieran gave me a wicked grin.

I was something all right.

7

"Will he be okay?" I asked. It wasn't the first time I'd posed the question, and unless someone gave me an answer, it wouldn't be my last.

Jase was lying on a couch in the main sitting room, cradling his shoulder. Issik had ripped off his shirt moments ago to get a better look at his injuries. The groan of pain from Jase's lips cut through me. We had made it back to the castle, but Jase wasn't out of the woods yet.

"The direhounds' fangs carry a poison that paralyzes their prey. It allows them to bring their hunt back to their den, and that's when the true torture begins," Issik explained while his fingers made quick work of assessing Jase's injuries.

A shiver ran down my spine. The thought of Jase being hunted like that—dragged back to a cave to be torn apart piece by piece—made my stomach churn. "It won't kill him?"

Issik examined the crimson scratches that ran down Jase's side. They were smooth marks, as if they'd been made with a blade instead of claws. "Depends on the amount of poison in his bloodstream, and how deep the bite is. If he had been bitten multiple times, it could have stopped his heart. Direhounds are lethal creatures, and not from the Veil."

I sat at the end of the coffee table Issik had pulled up to the couch, and my fingers gently stroked Jase's midnight hair. "They came through the portal?" I kept my voice low.

Beside me, Issik frowned, staring at his friend. "I'm afraid so."

"What is the point of breaking the curse that seals the portal if it lets in every nasty creature out there?" Frustration mingled with my worry for Jase.

Unable to sit still, Issik began to pace the room. "The problem is that without our full abilities, we can't close the portal, so it remains partially open. Tianna's curse is a magical beacon, attracting them. Once the curse is lifted, the signal will be gone."

And until then, we were supposed to somehow fend them off and search for the last star. Talk about making an absurd task impossible. The odds continued to be stacked against us.

Zade tended the fire at the front of the room, the crackling of wood filling the quiet room. Jase's golden complexion had become ashen as he drifted in and out of consciousness. "How long until the poison wears off?" I whispered.

Issik halted his pacing long enough to drag a hand through his hair. "Hours, but hopefully the antidote Kieran is making, will shorten the paralysis."

Jase moaned again.

I hated this feeling in my chest. It felt like my heart was going to plunge out of my rib cavity, and shatter into a million pieces. Jase's brow was damp with sweat, after a fever had consumed his body, and there was nothing I could do to help him.

Crouching down beside me, Issik took my hand, threading our fingers together. My eyes lifted to his, realizing he was watching me. The expression on his face was one of admiration and gratitude. "What you did out there... it was impressive. He might not have been here if you hadn't reacted. The poison works quick and hampered his ability to shift."

To be honest, I was doing my best to forget about what I had done. It wasn't the killing that bothered me, but that I had enjoyed the rush of magic—the power it gave me. "It doesn't seem real."

Lately, Issik and I were emotionally in sync, more so than the others. Sadness was a reoccurring theme in my life. He blinked, and calmness came into his eyes. "The guilt is normal, as is the relief at saving his life. It can be confusing."

"Is this the part where you tell me it gets easier?"

Was that a tiny smirk on his lips?

"I could lie to you and tell you it gets easier, but it doesn't. You have to learn to deal with it, to compartmentalize all the feelings, and trust in yourself."

I shook my head. "If only the emotions I felt stopped at guilt and relief. It's so complicated."

"Try me."

"A part of me liked it," I admitted with a heavy sigh. "Using magic, having power. I wasn't useless or afraid."

"You were never useless. Not to us," he assured. "Power

can be an addicting thing. You're smart to fear it, but also know it can be controlled. You don't have to let it control you."

My throat tightened, and I nodded, praying he was right.

Issik's lips pressed against my knuckles as he lifted my hand for a soft kiss. "Remind me not to piss you off," he murmured. "I would hate to go head to head with that flaming temper of yours."

His words coaxed a smile from me.

Kieran had given Jase the antidote, and he was sleeping soundly now—free of pain. The feverish sweat left his body, and I draped a throw over him. I lingered until he dozed off, while Zade slouched in a chair near the hearth, promising to watch over him through the night.

I retreated to my room with the sole purpose of bathing and sleeping. In that order. Discarding my clothes on the chair in the corner, I strolled into the bathroom in only my undergarments to turn on the water, waiting as it heated.

Why don't you heat it yourself? a voice purred in my head. *Why wait?* It was my voice talking, but it felt all kinds of wrong.

"Shut up," I hissed, rubbing at my temples.

Magic wasn't to be taken lightly or used on a whim, and right now, I wanted to forget I had any extraordinary abilities. I wanted to scrub away the tingle of power that radiated from my skin. I wanted a night of normalcy, and a bath with scented bubbles that foamed higher than the tub itself.

Slipping a hand in, I tested the water temperature and removed the last bits of my clothing. I let the water rush over my body as I stepped inside, and pure delight made a moan slip through my lips. Pink bubbles popped and snapped all around me, their rose scent tickling my nose.

I stared at my body, the rouge tint of my skin, and my hands. I didn't recognize them. Turning them over left to right, it was hard to believe what these hands were capable of. No signs of magic stained my fingertips, or revealed the flames that had morphed into a lethal weapon.

Gone was the girl I once knew, and I wasn't sure I liked who she was becoming.

My eyelids grew heavy as I allowed my body to relax. The heat of the water seeped into my muscles, but I refused to close my eyes. For in the darkness, the dire-hounds returned with their soulless eyes, and gleaming teeth. Yet, that wasn't all I saw. Even scarier was the woman who stood with her hair flying out like flames licking the air. Her bright eyes shone with ruthless anger, and whips of fire twined around her arms.

Her picture haunted me, refusing to leave me.

After soaking in the bath for nearly an hour, the chill that had resided in my veins finally dissolved, along with the bubbles. Stepping out, I found a cup of hot tea and cream on a tray in the sitting room, with an assortment of cookies. They were the best thing I'd ever tasted, and it piqued my hunger.

Bundled in a robe, I rubbed at my chest, at the empti-ness that wouldn't go away, and strolled to the bed. I picked up the Star of Persuasion and sat on top of the fluffy mattress, turning the stone over in my hands. Dying embers in the hearth washed the room in a soft light, and as I held up the stone, flecks of yellow and orange seemed to set the crystal afire.

Ancient power resided in this little stone. At first glance, it appeared dull and lifeless, but if you looked closer—really looked—you could see the beauty long since forgotten. It called to me, to my blood, and I longed to answer and make it whole once more. I could fight this feeling all I wanted, but it wouldn't change my destiny.

I was the keeper of the stars, the savior of dragons. I would do whatever it took to save them, including losing myself. If the price was my soul, I'd gladly give it.

In that acceptance, I finally found the peace I'd been seeking for days—or perhaps longer.

Slipping the crystal under my pillow, I lay down. Being in the chambers of Issik's mother made me feel protected. It didn't really make sense, but in a way, I felt closer to her, as if she would look out for me, even while I slept.

Perhaps it was the wards around the castle I was sensing, or being tucked away so remotely from the rest of the kingdoms. Regardless, there was a quiet in the air I found comforting. Jase was going to recover, and the knowledge lightened my heart.

With the fire glowing in my room, I closed my eyes and slept. No nightmares. No dreams. Just the soundless sleep my body so desperately needed.

The following evening, I found myself alone in my

bedroom. After sleeping until noon, I had spent most of the day keeping Jase company. He had gained much of his strength back, including the use of his tongue. By midday, he was barking orders to the staff, and grumbling about being treated like a baby instead of a king.

I was relieved to have the tranquility dragon alive and well, but this was another setback that cost us time—time we didn't have to lose. We all felt the hands of the clock ticking by, like a bomb about to explode in our faces.

Flipping the amber crystal in my hand, I stared at it, willing the thing to do something, give me a sign. It lay dormant between my fingers, dull and void of magic. I couldn't keep carrying it around with me; it was careless. The star might not have the power the others held, but it also wasn't just a stone. Therefore, it had to be protected. I couldn't explain it, but above all the rest, this star felt important, as if one day, it would shine again. Of course, the whole idea was absurd. I had too much fantasy in my real life, and I believed anything I dreamt up could happen.

Surveying my chambers, I became hell-bent on finding a spot in the suite to hide the stone. Under my pillow wasn't what I would call a safe or inventive location. If I were the witch, it would be the first place I'd look.

As I walked from room to room, I tapped my finger on my lip, eyeing the ornate knickknacks scattered over the dressers, shelves, and the fireplace mantel—a carved jewelry box, an ivory clock, and detailed sculptures. I rummaged through the hand-painted dressers and armoires, before looking at the vases filled with colored stones on top of the nightstands.

Hmm, I wonder…

Picking up one of the vases, I was surprised at its weight and was thankful I managed to hang on to the glass without dropping it. Raw-cut crystals of milky white, rose quartz, and one eerily similar to the Star of Persuasion were inside. The idea of hiding the star in the vase held promise, but as I chewed on my lip, I realized it would be easy to forget which one was indeed the Star of Persuasion.

My search continued. When had I become so bad at hiding things? Living on the streets, it had been an everyday occurrence—stashing my belongings where no one else would find or steal them. Now, I couldn't even stow a crystal out of sight.

Pathetic.

Refusing to give up, I turned my attention to the hearth. Was it possible there was a loose brick in the stone surrounding the fireplace? It worked in the movies. It seemed like a longshot, but what did I have to lose? Running my hands along the wall, I pushed and knocked at the bricks. This was stupid, and it proved to be a waste of my time. The hearth was solid.

I leaned a hand against the mantel and stared at the elaborate, silk-draped bed, wondering if I should slice a hole in the mattress. My nose scrunched at the idea of destroying something so beautiful, and that had belonged to a queen. I couldn't do it.

A ray of moonlight, softly streaming through a small crack between the ice blue curtains, called my attention. I traced the line to where it landed on an ivory statue sitting above the mantel, just a few inches from my hand. A female with full curves was swept up in a wave at her feet. Upon closer inspection, I realized she had pointed ears like an elf. Her face was young and beautiful. The long strands of her hair blew in an eternal breeze. The wave beneath her was supported by an oval base just big enough to hide the Star of Persuasion under it.

It was a fleeting thought, but my skin tingled, and I swore the crashing of the sea wave echoed in my ears. Compelled to pick up the statue, I wrapped my fingers around the cool stone, just as a draft blew down from the flue, causing the orange flames to sway.

What is going on?

Would anything normal ever happen to me again?

I tried to pick up the statue from her perch on the mantel, intent on inspecting the base, but to my surprise, she wouldn't budge. Repositioning my grip, I tried again and noticed something odd. I could twist her, so I did. She made a complete circle before clicking to a stop. The slab of brick in front of me groaned, and small pebbles crumbled to the ground.

What the—

The outline of a rectangle broke through the bricks, opening a sliver to reveal a secret door. Could this be real?

Releasing the statue, I let my fingers trace the rough outline, needing proof it wasn't a trick of the eye. The bricks were jagged and coarse under my touch. I should have alerted one of the descendants of my find, but my curiosity urged me to take a peek, I needed to see what was behind the door.

Leaning my shoulder into the bricks, I shoved against the door, and it swung open, revealing a dark passage on the other side. From the black depths, a stale breeze blew over my face, twirling the strands of my hair. My dragons should know better than to leave me alone, even if only for a night. This was going to lead to all kinds of trouble.

I glanced back into the room, at the ruffled bed, at the clothes strewn over the chair, at the door leading to the sitting area. If I took a step into the tunnel, what would I find?

"Olivia..." a soft voice called, disappearing like a shooting star through the night sky.

My head whipped back toward the opening in the wall, and at the same time, the Star of Persuasion pulsed in my hand. I opened my palm and stared down at the stone. Its center burned brightly, in rhythmic beats.

Interesting.

One thing was clear, it wanted me to go into the tunnel, to find whatever waited for me down there.

Going with my gut, I took a single step through the door, and unless my eyes were suddenly playing tricks on me, I saw the star beat faster. Excitement rippled through me alongside a dash of unease. Using the light emitting from the star, I held it out in front of me, and moved deeper down the passage. A staircase appeared not too far from the entrance, the steps under my feet seemed very old and went on forever. From the cobwebs tangling in my hair, and the things that scurried away at my approach, this tunnel hadn't been used in years—decades, more likely.

A chill hung in the air, but considering where I was in the Veil, that wasn't surprising. Did Issik's wards extend to this part of the castle?

My footsteps were light and cautious, the only sound in the eerie quiet. The deeper I traveled, the darker it became until I was surrounded by nothing but stark midnight, and with it, came those ugly nightmares I longed to forget. My breathing quickened.

You're not trapped in a box. You're not a prisoner, I reminded myself. *You're free. You're safe. You're powerful.*

Hold up. I halted. I was powerful. I did have abilities, so why wasn't I using them? The Star of Fire might be gone, but the magic of the stone lived inside me. I proved it yesterday when I had taken down those direhounds, but my confidence in wielding magic wasn't without concerns. My abilities had changed, and I couldn't say if it was because of Tianna or the combination of the stars. I had no choice but to learn to control it… or be controlled by it.

Letting the burn of fire roar through my blood, I snapped my fingers, and a ball of flames flickered over my hand like a torch. The warm glow heated my face, but didn't harm my flesh. Wicked cool. Perhaps having magic wasn't all bad. A smile tugged at the corner of my mouth, and I continued my descent.

Once I reached the bottom, I rotated the star left to right, watching it flicker at different intervals. Before me were four paths—each identically dark and dusty. It was hard not to think about the spiders and rats that might call this underground home. A shudder rolled through me.

I am not afraid. I am not afraid. I am not afraid, I chanted over and over again.

"Olivia…"

The echo of my name reached me from one of the tunnels, in a female voice that caressed me as a mother's touch would. I could be walking into one of Tianna's traps. It could be her voice luring me into the dark, but that didn't explain the sudden weird behavior of the stone in my hand.

My human ears couldn't detect which tunnel the voice had come from, unfortunately. So, using slow movements, I scanned the amber crystal over each opening and chose one of the paths on the right, based on the increased pulses of the stone. "I hope you know what you're doing," I mumbled to the star.

With each step, the passage grew colder and dampness chilled the air. A drop of water hitting the stone floor echoed from somewhere in front of me. The flames over my fingers sputtered, but I pressed on, letting the stone be my guide.

How much would it suck if I got lost down here? Would the star also lead me out?

I passed multiple round doorways and other passages, but the star continued to navigate me straight.

Soon, an arched door came into view with a silver dragon standing proud on its hind legs, emblazoned on the wood. A blue light shone from under the door and onto the stones. My teeth gnawed at the inside of my cheek, considering my options. If I opened this door, I couldn't take back what I found—good or bad. I would have to deal with what lay behind the unique passage alone.

The sputtering flame at my fingers extinguished as I closed my fist. Between the luminous amber stone and the light under the door, I didn't need my fire to see.

As I placed my hand on the metal handle, a gust caused the hairs on my arms to stand up and my skin to prickle. The cool breeze carried the whisper of my name once more, and my blood hummed as if what was behind the door called to me. Was it the Star of Frost? Had I found it so quickly?

Pressing down, the handle clicked, and I gave the door a shove. Dust sprinkled from the hinges, getting into my eyes and nostrils. Briefly, I turned my face into my inner elbow, and coughed before taking a step forward into the unknown.

The smell was the first thing I noticed. It reminded me of lotuses at midnight, an odd scent for an unused section of the castle. Glittering jewels greeted my stunned face. A treasure room? Was that what this was? Beautiful tapestries and paintings hung on the walls. Crowns, tiaras, necklaces, golden goblets, pearls, and so many other dazzling possessions covered the space.

In the center of the room was a desk with papers scattered on top, and I went over to get a closer look. It was a stack of maps, and places I'd never heard of in my life. Thumbing through the pile, I realized they must be other worlds. Ellemere. Hyren. Tulans. Larken, and so many more. A million questions spun in my head.

Would the portal—when opened—allow us to travel to these worlds? Did they all really exist? Who lived there?

A candelabra sat on the left corner of the desk, and I waved my hand over the top of the used wicks, lighting the three tapered candles. Firelight bathed the desk, casting shadows over the maps.

"You like history?" A light, female voice rang behind me.

8

I jumped, my heart hammering in my chest, and as I whirled around, my leg banged against one of the desk's wooden legs. Pain radiated from my knee, and I cursed, letting out a string of swear words.

A woman in white stood before me, clearer and more lifelike than any of her sisters had appeared to be. I was tempted to lift my hand and touch her, to know if she felt as real as she looked.

"Such a temper," she mused lightheartedly, with a twist to her lips. "It will serve you well for what is to come."

"It's you," I breathed, the air rushing out of my lungs in relief. Oh, thank God it wasn't the witch.

"I am Eira, the former queen of Iculon, and I have something for you, Olivia." She was as stunning as I remembered, her silver hair flowing down her back like a waterfall of starlight. Her crystal blue eyes twinkled.

"Is it the Star of Frost?" I tried to keep the hopefulness from my tone, failing miserably.

"Not quite," she replied, the humor vanishing from her eyes. "But it will be of importance one day, and it is imperative you keep it safe, keep it hidden. In the wrong hands, this item could be destructive not only to this world, but all worlds."

"What is it?" I asked. Could I really be trusted to keep another crucial item safe? Did I want that responsibility? Not that it mattered. I wouldn't refuse a request from the spirit of a dead queen, who had way more knowledge about this world than I did.

The queen reached into a wooden chest in the corner of the room, and pulled out a cloth-wrapped, rectangular package. "You must not share the contents of this with anyone—not until the time is right."

God, I hated secrets. "How will I know when that is?"

"You will know," she insisted, not answering my question in that annoying way the women in white did. A glimmer of pride shone in her eyes. "You've changed. There is a light about you, a glow of magic beyond the dragon stones."

I nodded, my stomach pitching. "The witch took the Star of Fire. I'm so sorry. I tried to stop her—"

She silenced me with a look. "It is not your fault, daughter. You do not owe me an apology. Everything that happens has a purpose, even if you don't understand it at the moment."

Was she telling me that Tianna was supposed to take the Star of Fire, because in doing so, I would be granted a seed of magic? I didn't pretend to understand the workings of fate, if I even believed in it. "I don't understand."

"Take this." She pushed the dusty package into my hands, her soft fingers covering mine, felt very real and very cold. "Now, go before something picks up your scent."

The package was heavier than it appeared, like I held a textbook in my hands. "Wait!" I called out before she disappeared on me. "Who would pick up my scent?" The sudden change in her eyes, to what looked like fear, had my heart racing.

"There are things in this world, creatures searching for you, and if they get a whiff of your power, these tunnels won't be safe for you."

I worked through what she was telling me. I already knew of the creatures slipping through the portals, but how would they get into the tunnels? Unless... "Are you saying there is a portal down here?"

"That is exactly what I'm telling you, daughter. Although my body is stronger here, I cannot stay long. Neither can you. It isn't safe to be outside the wards of the castle. Now, hurry." A ripple of something unearthly and cold traveled through the air.

Her eyes went wide, and she took ahold of my shoulders, pushing me toward the open door. "Run, quickly! Do not waver! Do not lose your way!"

A gust of wind surged down the hallway, kicking up dust and blowing my hair back from my face. The faint sound of something close to a growl had my feet moving before my mind could tell them. I didn't look back to check if Queen Eira lingered, regardless of how much I wanted to see her one last time. Flicking out my hand, I summoned fire, and ran back the way I had come.

I didn't stop running. Not even when I came to the endless stairs, or when I stumbled more than once going up the staircase. I didn't let up my pace until I hurled myself through the secret door, into my room, and slammed it shut behind me.

Remembering the statue, I twisted the ivory woman counterclockwise until the lock clicked into place once again. Only then did I allow myself a moment. Slouching against the sealed wall, my breaths came out in hard pants, the cloth-wrapped package still clutched to my chest.

Dropping it onto the bed, along with the star, I walked to the bathroom to splash cold water on my face. My heart was still racing, and the face staring back at me in the mirror was bone white. My hands shook as they gripped the side of the basin. *A portal. In the tunnels.* I didn't want to fathom what that meant.

After cleaning myself up and removing the spider webs that had clung to my hair, I sat on the bed, eyeing the wrapped bundle. I had more or less stopped panting, but my heart rate had yet to return to normal. Seeing what was swaddled in cloth, and an inch of grime, probably wouldn't help, but that didn't stop me from unwrapping the package.

Dust and dirt transferred onto the lush duvet, tarnishing its beauty as I peeled back the cloth, trying not to be disgusted. I made a face, crinkling my nose against the stale smell that lingered in the air from the dust. Crumpling the fabric, I tossed the ball into the hearth, and watched the flames burst to life once the material caught fire.

My gaze returned to my bed to behold a book, so I picked it up, laying it on my lap. Why would Queen Eira give me a book? Was there something inside to break the curse or stop Tianna? It seemed and felt ancient, like something that didn't belong in mortal hands.

I wiped off the cover, revealing the title embossed in silver lettering—The Book of Stars.

Holy shit.

Was this what I thought it was? A book about the dragon stones? Could it be? Did such a thing exist?

My fingers ran along the spine, tracing the thick leather cover. Silver lined the edges of the pages, and I swore the book was singing to me. A song with words I couldn't understand whispered into my ears—a deep and slow melody full of mystery and enchantment. The Star of Persuasion lay on the bed, pulsing with the song as if it were answering its summons.

I was afraid to touch the crystal. Would it be warm? Alive with restored power? Or was I being fanciful and foolish?

As I opened the book, a tingle slid down my spine, and I rubbed the goosebumps on my arms, scanning the first page. An embossed illustration of a silver tree with exposed roots wove down the page. The roots branched off into five different tendrils, each encircling a symbol—tranquility, poison, fire, frost, and persuasion.

Hours passed while I flipped through the pages. The book was written in a divine script I'd never seen before, which made it impossible to read. Notes had been scribbled along the margins, but even then, it made little sense to me. The plethora of drawings and pictures were what kept me mesmerized.

What was in this particular book that the women in white wanted me to find? I understood why they wouldn't want something of this magnitude in the hands of a witch like Tianna. The knowledge within this book would give her more power and ammunition than one human, witch, or anyone should ever have.

However, wasn't it all irrelevant if I didn't find the Star of Frost? Not to mention, I had to recover the Star of Fire from Tianna's greedy clutches. Did I really need to worry about what was inside the Book of Stars too? Had the women in white led me to the secret tunnels, and the treasure room, at this moment for a reason?

The unanswered questions were endless.

And the dangers...

A phantom breeze flowed through the room, carrying the distinct scent of lotuses. I shivered despite the warm fire beside me.

Now, I needed a hiding place big enough for the star *and* the book. I had thought it was problematic before... I clutched the book to my chest and the stone in my hand before kneeling to peer under the bed. Grasping at straws, I desperately searched for somewhere to stash the magical objects entrusted to my care. Why would anyone think I was capable of protecting something of this importance? I couldn't walk and chew gum at the same time!

"Where the hell have you been?" Boomed a voice from the doorway.

I jerked in surprise, bumping my damn head on the bed at the sudden intrusion. Swearing under my breath, I shoved the book and the stone in a dark alcove under the bed and turned to rise, rubbing the sore spot on the back of my head. On my feet, I faced a cross-armed, glowering Jase, and steeled myself for the bitch fest that was sure to come.

"Do you have to sneak up on me all the time? Make some blasted noise when you come into a room. Or, here's a thought, knock," I barked, not bothering to hide the annoyance in my tone.

His eyes narrowed. "What were you doing under there?"

"Glad to see you're feeling better." I was avoiding the question.

"I came to your room earlier. You can imagine my surprise when I found it empty."

Keeping my expression blank, I shrugged and smoothed invisible wrinkles from my dress. "I was restless and went for a walk." It was true. I just omitted the details about the walk being through a passage of secret tunnels.

"Hmm." Jase pursed his lips, clearly suspicious. "What trouble are you up to?"

I rolled my eyes. "Why am I always the one who is up to no good?"

He lifted an arrogant brow. "Does that question deserve a reply?"

My lips became a thin line. "You're so lucky you're recovering from a near-death experience."

"You know, I'm feeling much better." His hand shot out, snatching my wrist and tugging me against him.

My palms flattened against his chest while I peered up at him with a sparkle in my eye. "Is that so?" Flirting with Jase was safer than him interrogating me. Something about his eyes, and the way he gazed at me as if he could see my soul, made it difficult to keep myself from spilling my guts. He had a way about him that made me want to share everything, to lean on him, to open myself up completely.

"You know, I had it under control."

I snorted. "Not from where I stood. You scared me. I didn't like it."

"Now you understand how I feel, but I suppose I ought to show you my thanks." He pressed a kiss to the sensitive spot just under my ear, causing a shudder to roll through me. I tilted my head to the side, giving him unobstructed access to my neck, and he flicked his tongue over my skin. "I love the way you taste," he murmured, nipping at my ear.

Slipping my fingers into his hair, I let my eyes flutter closed. Jase's kisses held their own kind of magic, and each caress melted my bones, turning my core into molten lava. "Are you ever going to kiss me?"

He chuckled, sending goosebumps running down my throat. "Good things come to those who wait," he whispered, tracing my jaw with his lips.

"I'm not a patient person." And to drive the point home, I snuck my wandering fingers under his shirt, gliding my nails over his hard abs. I was rewarded as they rippled from my touch. I wanted my lips on him.

Jase's fingers threaded through my hair, tipping my face up to meet his gaze. A hunger lit those violet eyes as they fixated on my lips, our breaths mingling. "So I've noticed." He dipped his head, and I waited, poised on the edge for that mouth to meet mine, but he skirted to the side, kissing the corner of my lips.

"What kind of thanks is this?" I pouted.

"Let me show you."

Leaning down, he pressed his lips to mine in a kiss that shook the world. His mouth was sultry, soft, and warm. Jase Dior. The dragon who had whisked me off the streets of Chicago. The heir with dreamy violet eyes and a roguish smirk. I felt as if I'd waited since meeting him for this moment, and my restraint slipped away. I needed all of him. Now. And if the damn dragon attempted to leave me with just a few kisses and teasing touches, I was going to make him wish I hadn't saved his sorry ass.

I couldn't kiss him enough. He was the most potent drug in the world. Each kiss made me want more, and more, and more. A potent need rushed through me, and he growled softly into my mouth.

"Jase." His name came out as a whimper, a prayer, and a curse.

Skilled fingers ran down to the small of my arched back and somehow slipped the straps of my dress off my shoulders at the same time. The cool temperature of the room drifted over my exposed skin as the material fell to my hips. His fingers explored unabashedly over the planes of my belly, his lips slowing down with each touch.

The change in tempo made my head spin. From hot and fast to slow and gentle. I couldn't catch my breath, nor could I keep up with the sensations rocking my body. And then his hand rose up to stroke under the swell of my breasts, and I trembled, aching to feel his touch there. My body responded to him like a minstrel strumming the strings of a harp, creating something beautiful and enchanting.

I pushed him down onto the bed. Not only could I no longer stand on my legs, but I longed to feel him closer. Straddling him, I sunk my body onto his, the blond waves of my hair falling in a curtain around us.

My fingers fumbled with the button on his pants, while my lips teased the muscles of his bare chest. I wanted the barriers between us gone, to feel all the dips and curves of my body flush against his—that perfect fit between male and female.

In one swift predatory motion, Jase flipped our positions, and I savored the weight of him pressed into me. His body was warm and solid. His smoky purple eyes filled with a ravenous desire to travel the length of my torso. I watched as his gaze devoured my peaked breasts, before he dipped his head, and took one into his mouth.

My back bowed, coming off the bed. *God, he'd been worth the wait. So worth it.* The dragon of calm and peace was none of those traits as a lover. I became aware of every place those lips roamed, from the outer curve of my ear to the inside of my thigh.

Suddenly, he paused, and my eyes fluttered open. "Why did you stop?" I asked huskily, ready to bare my teeth at him.

"I just need a moment to look at you. I want to see you when I'm inside of you."

The core of my passion tightened in response to his words. I had to have him. All of him. Now.

I reached for him, and his fingers cradled my hips as he nudged himself at the opening of my center. My eyes were caught by the vibrant violet of his, and I stopped breathing, waiting, and waiting. My hips drew up, pushing the tip of him inside the warmth of me, but he held back. Biting my lip, I groaned. A wild, almost feral hunger swept over his features in response, and still, he took his sweet time torturing me.

The muscles bunched on his arms, as his eyes simmered. "I don't like sharing. Not what is mine. And make no mistake, Cupcake, you're mine." His teeth dragged over my lower lip. "Now, and for as long as I shall live."

What did that mean? I didn't get the opportunity to pry for more details. His lips were on mine again in a deep, drugging kiss that demanded all of my attention, and wiped every thought from my mind.

We were a tangle of limbs, kisses, and teeth. Heart to heart our bodies joined, and the world drifted away, leaving just Jase and I intertwined in my silky sheets.

9

I lay wrapped in Jase's arms, happily exhausted, sweaty, and smelling of him. A comfortable silence fell between us for a spell before he made love to me again. It was as sweet and smoldering as the first time.

My fingers drew lazy circles around his heart, and my thoughts turned to how only a day before he'd been poisoned by the direhounds. It was an image that would haunt me for years, seeing him unable to move or speak, seeing his body fight the venom of the beasts. "You could have died, you know."

Trailing up and down my arm, his fingers paused at the sound of my voice. Glancing downward, he gave me an arrogant grin. "I didn't though, thanks to you."

"Luck. That was dumb luck."

"When are you going to accept that you're amazing? I don't even think Tianna had any idea what she was unleashing when she cast that spell. If she had an inkling of the girl who would one day break our curse, she might have had second thoughts about wrecking her evil on the Veil and double-crossing the kings."

I laughed—a short sound that came out as part snort. "We haven't beaten her yet."

Jase kissed the tip of my nose. "No, but we will."

His sheer confidence in me, in our survival, was inspiring. He made me believe it. "I love you," I whispered, nestling my head into the crook of his arm.

"Not nearly as much as I love you." His fingers combed through my hair with each word.

A calmness I hadn't felt in a long time settled over me, allowing me to drift easily into sleep, but that was where the tranquility ended.

My dreamworld placed me in a long corridor lined with Grecian columns that shone gold under the sun's rays. Water trickled in the distance, and the air was perfumed with a bouquet of magnolias, freesias, and sweet peas from the vibrant gardens around me. The air was toasty and caressed my skin while I strolled through the hall, my heels clicking on the paved pathway.

I wore a flowing white toga that barely covered the important bits. The sheer fabric moved with the wind, exposing a large portion of my thighs, but I didn't care. In fact, I enjoyed the provocative attire and the attention I received. Gold bangles clanged together on my wrists, and my fingers were adorned with rings that refracted the light as I studied my hand.

Since when did I have a birthmark on my wrist? A crescent moon marked the inside of my arm.

It was then I realized this wasn't my body... or my thoughts.

My footsteps faltered, and I barely avoided colliding with a column in my confusion.

Behind me, a rich and sultry woman laughed. "When has my sister become so clumsy?"

My spine locked into place at the sound of that voice. It was one I would never forget, not for as long as I lived, and I had a feeling it would plague me long after I was gone. "Tianna," I whispered, but the voice that came out of my mouth wasn't mine. It was softer, and full of admiration for the woman approaching me.

I turned, and my heart felt like it had been ripped out of my chest in one quick jerk.

Tianna paused in front of me, a smile twisting her berry-stained lips. "Were you expecting someone else, dear sister? A lover perhaps?" Her mocking tone suggested Tianna's sister didn't have many lovers, and Tianna's spiteful grin implied she would have been jealous if that had been the case.

"What do you need, Tianna?" the sister I embodied asked in mild annoyance, as if she was upset her peace had been interrupted. I got the feeling the witch sisters didn't always get along.

"I need your help."

"I told you. I'm not going to get involved. I have no desire to rule the world."

"Corvina," Tianna dragged out her sister's name. "I can't do this without you." Her calculating look turned into pleading puppy eyes.

I could feel Corvina's resolve weakening piece by piece, and all I wanted to do was scream at her. "You underestimate your own abilities. We both know you don't need my help."

"Perhaps," Tianna conceded. "But are you willing to let me take the chance? The dragons have called for aid. This is the moment we've been waiting for—a chance to reinstate magic where it belongs, and the dragon stars will give us that opportunity. Don't you want to feel what our ancestors had before magic was contained?"

"I doubt the dragon kings are going to hand over the ancient stars, just because you said please." Corvina spun the rings on her fingers as she replied.

"They will if they want our help to end this war. And I don't need them all. Just one... or two," she added, tapping a long, onyx nail against her lips. The grin on her face made me want to throat punch her. Lies. Lies. Lies.

Corvina knew her sister wouldn't quit, not when she got an idea in her head. She would harp, beg, and connive until she got what she desired. It was her way. And she still loved her sister. "If I go with you to the Veil Isles, this is the last thing you ask of me. I want no part of what you do after."

Tianna looped her arm through Corvina's, flashing her teeth in a wicked smile. "Deal."

Corvina didn't really believe her sister. She knew Tianna would never be satisfied. Not even after she obtained the power she coveted, but Corvina had plans of her own. She wanted to leave Mistaven—her home. She'd had enough of her sister's schemes, and longed for a life of her own making. Of love and children. Of happiness.

The dream shifted, and with it, the cries and screams of war raged around me. When the mist faded, I caught the glint of steel slicing through the air. The world was still hazy, blurring the face in control of the broad sword. I didn't have time to leap out of the way —or Corvina didn't—but at the last second, before the blade struck its mark, Corvina raised her staff. The edge of the sword sunk into the wood, and she hissed at the impact vibrating through her arms.

Grunting, she ripped the staff free from the sword, putting a step or two of space between her and the assailant. I squinted, trying to make out the shape of the face. A nudge of recognition poked at me, but it remained out of my grasp.

My heart thundered in my ears as the magic in Corvina's

veins flickered. She knew she had to end this quickly. Her powers were wavering, leaving her to rely on training and determination alone. She fought like a skilled assassin, deflecting blow after blow with her staff.

To be inside her body, inside her mind, was staggering and empowering. This was how it felt to be a badass, to know how to truly wield magic.

An intoxicating feeling rushed through me so powerfully that my body sang. Corvina unleashed a burst of magic that slammed into her attacker, giving her a few breaths to regain her composure, but it wasn't long enough.

Darkness passed over the golden sun, and in that instant, Corvina and I both knew death was on the horizon. Sadness and regret mixed in Corvina's blood with her waning magic. She lifted her staff while sparks of power danced off her fingertips, preparing herself... but it was too late.

The sword swung again, a golden light erupting from the thin edge of the blade, and whooshing toward me.

It sunk into its mark, and I glanced down to see the glowing sword sticking out of my chest. The taste of something hot and acidic hit my tongue, while my blood oozed from the entry sight, soaking the fabric of my ivory war armor. My breath slowed, becoming irregular.

"What have you done?" Corvina wheezed, dropping to her knees. The pain finally registered, soaring through my heart. Agony had me screaming before I flew backward and hit the ground with a sickening thud.

This isn't real, I reminded myself. *It is a dream... or a vision. I'm not dying. I am not Corvina.*

The reminder did little to ease the pain. Tears stung my eyes as I looked up into the face of Corvina's killer. Her features *came into focus—a beautiful face with creamy skin, flaming red hair, and silver eyes that glistened like stars.*

"Tianna," Corvina gasped, blood trickling from the corner of her mouth, and I shivered at the sensation, it was so real.

Tianna had killed her own sister.

"Corvina," Tianna sobbed, dropping down beside her sister's bleeding body. "Forgive me."

"Why?" I gurgled, blood filling my lungs. It was the last thing Corvina ever said—a question that followed her into the afterlife.

I woke up gasping. My accelerated breathing was so harsh that my lungs strained. A sharp pang suddenly radiated from my chest, causing my hand to fly to my heart. I sighed out loud when I touched my cool skin. No blade. No blood. No death.

I was alive and unharmed. It was only a twisted dream of the past—Corvina's past.

Tianna's silence over the last week made me anxious, and this dream… it only solidified my fears. She was up to something, and I didn't dare let myself wonder what, or how bad it would be when she finally came out of her wicked cave.

How could she have killed her own sister? That took a special kind of monster.

The pain ebbed, but the memory of the dream lingered for hours, and not even the warmth of Jase's arms could banish the darkness from my mind.

I staggered into the kitchen with Jase behind me, and plopped into one of the high-backed chairs. A breakfast large enough to feed an army was laid out on the table. A cup of coffee was placed in front of me, and I grumbled a thank you before splashing creamer in, followed by heaps of sugar.

Kieran sent me a lopsided grin. "You're perky today."

Huffing, I gulped down half the contents of my mug. Some people sipped their coffee. I inhaled it. "Forgive me for not waking up with rainbows shooting from my eyes. Not all of us are morning people."

Kieran's grin only grew.

"The nightmares still keep you up?" Zade guessed from across the table, where he watched me with a perceptive eye.

Hating the insight they had into my subconscious, I sighed. Yes, the dream had kept me up, but it had also been my little venture into the tunnels, and Jase that had me all out of sorts this morning. The book I'd found was still shoved under my bed, and I was itching to do something with it. No clue what exactly, but the women in white had led me to it for a reason, and I owed it to them, to the descendants, and to myself to figure out what inside the book was so important.

"It's nothing I can't handle," I replied, staring into my cup and doing my best to pretend it was no big deal.

Yet, the secrets I was keeping were taking a toll. I hated the lies, even the ones by omission. It felt wrong, and I fooled no one, least of all the descendants. They had a pipeline to my emotions, so it was ridiculous to think I could hide how I truly felt.

"No one said you couldn't, but you don't have to. There are other ways," Zade offered.

"What sort of other—" I stopped myself from asking. The answer came to me before I finished. "You mean having Jase knock me out?" I slid the tranquility dragon a long side glance. He showed no reaction to the conversation, and went about his business filling his plate.

Zade shrugged, propping the side of his face on a fist. "Why do you make it sound like a bad thing? There is no shame in using our abilities for good. Not everything in our lives is about killing. Actually, before the war, our lands had been peaceful for decades."

"I didn't mean to sound ungrateful. I guess I'm still wary of magic." Particularly when the minuscule amount I had inside me was unpredictable. I didn't know what to do with it, or how it made me feel. In truth, magic frightened me. Not the actual use of magic, but the craving for more it instilled within me.

"No one will fault you for that. It is easy to forget you didn't always know magic existed," Jase offered beside me.

"Didn't you stay with her last night?" Kieran asked Jase nonchalantly, but there was no mistaking the insinuation in his emerald eyes.

Stabbing one of the sausages, I lifted it onto my plate. "Your point?" I hated the color that bloomed on my cheeks, giving away everything.

Giving me a lazy grin, he shrugged. "Explains the shitty mood. If I had to wake up to his brooding face, I'd be as surly as a starving wolf."

I rolled my eyes. "I assure you, Jase isn't the cause." My gaze met his violet next to me.

A round of snickers ensued, even Issik joined them,

and the color on my face deepened. Nothing I said would help the situation, so I just kept my mouth shut.

Jase scowled. "As enlightening as this conversation has been, we have other matters to discuss. The direhounds we fought the other day, are just the beginning of the creatures that will be lured into our world."

The sweet taste of mango engulfed my tongue as I bit into it, as I thought about what I'd learned last night. There was a portal in the secret tunnels of Iculon Keep. That could be problematic *and* dangerous. However, if I told the descendants, they would definitely want to know how I'd come to learn of such information, which would lead to a slew of questions I wasn't sure I could answer—including the fact I'd been conversing with their dead mothers. So, I continued to shove food into my mouth, to keep from saying anything.

Leaning forward on the table, Kieran held a cup of something that definitely wasn't coffee in his hand. "If we could find a way to monitor the portal, we could stop them at the gate."

"It might make a difference in whatever battle lies ahead. We know Tianna isn't going to freely leave the Veil once the curse has been lifted," Issik tightly added. "And do we really want her to?"

Jase's fingers drummed on the wooden tabletop with the question. "The first thing we need to do is seal the portal. No one leaves. And then we deal with the witch."

Issik's face was a hardened mask when he glanced at us. "Our abilities won't be hampered by her curse any longer. She won't be able to take us all on."

"She managed to manipulate our fathers a century ago," Jase reminded us as a caution. The witch was cunning. No one believed she didn't have another agenda at play. Her thirst for the stars, for power, wouldn't end with the curse. That much we could guarantee.

Zade was quiet for a moment, his fingers clenching, unclenching, and clenching again. "Right now, our top priority is finding the last stone, and killing any creature that doesn't belong here. As long as the portal is ajar, our world is in danger. We need the last star."

All eyes fell on me, and I winced, the fork between my fingers freezing midway to my mouth.

"How are you feeling?" Kieran asked. The tattoo on his arm flashed from under the sleeve of his shirt as he crossed his arms.

His was a twofold question. "I'm fine," I insisted. Other than the nightmares, that was mostly true. "But I haven't had any inclination to where the last stone might be. Not yet," I said, predicting what they all were dying to know. The pressure was on. As long as the portal was open—even a sliver—the Veil was vulnerable.

Perhaps this was all part of the witch's master plan. The curse. The stars. The portal. The creatures. Destroy the Veil. Destroy the dragons. Gain a slice of the power of the gods.

The dancing snowflakes that fell from the late afternoon sky held my gaze, while I sat curled up on the center of my bed. A few days had passed by with little activity, which should have been good, but I couldn't figure out why it made me so rattled.

It could also be that Mother Nature had decided to curse me today with my monthly cycle. I stretched across the bed to grab the cup of hot tea that Juniper had brought me a few minutes ago, and winced at the pain slicing through my lower abdomen. Cramps were the devil. I breathed through the pain, my fingers digging into the duvet, and I swore under my breath.

I should be grateful. However cruddy and horrid I felt, it meant I wasn't pregnant. I couldn't imagine having a baby at my age, or in this world, with the cruelty of the witch who wished to rule over it. Not to mention, which descendant would be the father? Talk about a colossal fight in the works.

The tea was laced with a natural pain reliever. Juniper had informed me it would help ease the cramps. What I wouldn't do for a bottle of aspirin right about now. I glanced down at the cup. *Juniper, you better be right.* And drank half of it, eager to have the herbs kick in and fix me.

While lying in a fetal position, I noticed Jase show up to darken my doorway. My eyes flicked in his direction, shooting him an evil look only a woman could understand. He was dressed from head to toe in black—I called them his ninja clothes. The sleeves were cut off to showcase the strength of his arms, and he looked ready for battle.

"What are you doing still in bed, and why aren't you dressed? I waited ten minutes for you." We had resumed training yesterday—much to my dismay—but at the moment, the idea of moving at all made me groan. Jase, however, wasn't happy. Ten whole minutes was a lifetime for the punctual dragon.

"Training has been canceled for the day," I informed, shaking my head. "There is no way you are getting me out of this room. I'm taking a sick day."

Instant concern entered his eyes, and he crossed the room, sitting on the edge of the bed. His cool fingers pressed to my forehead. "You're ill?"

"Calm down." I swatted at his hand. "I'm not sick in that way. I'm… indisposed. That's all you need to know."

Lines creased over his brow as he continued to stare down at me. "Juniper mentioned you were unwell."

"I'm not sick," I emphasized, wondering how many times I had to say it before it got through his thick skull.

Jase's eyes narrowed as he looked me over. "You're not quitting on me, are you?"

Tugging on the blanket, I pulled it up to my chin. "Can't a girl just have a day to herself?" I huffed, nothing I said seemed to satisfy him or make the dragon leave me alone. Couldn't he see or sense my reluctance? Maybe it was Zade's connection that alerted them to my short temper and misery.

"What's wrong? You seem moodier than usual."

"You have no idea," I grumbled, picking at a loose string on the bed.

His fingers brushed a strand of hair off my forehead. "Well, if you're not truly sick, then there is no reason we can't do some drills. Perhaps we could take the day off from combat and work with your abilities, test your body to see how it is holding up with the three powers."

"You really are a hard ass, you know that? I'm tempted to tranquilize you."

His brows rose.

"I assumed with your expertise of women, that you'd be able to tell when it's *that* time of the month."

That stunned him. No more talk about training came from his full lips, and for the first time, Jase's cheeks grew red. He actually blushed in embarrassment. "Oh."

It was difficult to hide my smile at his sudden awkwardness. I took guilty pleasure in making the descendants squirm, which I hadn't expected to enjoy doing, like poking a bruise. I laughed lightly. "You should see your face." It was a memory I planned to tuck away for the next time I needed a good laugh.

"Um, if you need anything..." he stuttered, forking a hand through his obsidian hair.

God, could he look any more adorable? "I'm fine," I assured him. "I just need an entire plate of brownies, and some more of Juniper's tea."

Pleased to have an excuse to leave, he couldn't have

jumped at the opportunity faster. "I'll have the cook whip you up a batch." And he would, I realized, because I had asked, and he wanted to make me happy.

"Thanks, Jase."

Bowing his head, he quickly exited my room with less stealth than he had arrived. I swore I heard him bump into a chair and curse under his breath before the room went silent, and I was once again alone. Geez, you'd think I had the plague, but at least the cramps had subsided for the time being. Juniper's brew of tea had done the trick.

The descendants took turns poking their heads in throughout the day, inquiring if there was anything I desired, but for the most part, they left me to nurse my cramps and let Juniper take care of me. Their concern was cute but unnecessary, as if they didn't quite know what to do around me. For all the females in their life, they really could have used some sisters. I still had the plate of brownies I'd requested earlier, but had already polished off two.

Snowflakes glistened on the window panes, sticking to the glass as the snow began to fall with gusto. I wiped the crumbs from the corners of my mouth and slid off the mattress to dig out the book hidden under the bed along with the Star of Persuasion. I'd been aching to take another peek inside, since I'd found the Book of Stars days ago, but the opportunity to do so alone hadn't presented itself until now.

Taking the book and the stone into the sitting room, I dropped them both onto the table as I took a seat. It was as I remembered, ancient, heavy, and alluring. My fingers ran over the leather jacket, tracing the symbol etched into the cover. The ink seemed to glimmer under my touch, and tingles pranced down my arm, warming my blood.

Magic calls to magic.

I didn't know where the words had come from. They were just there, echoing in my head, and ringing with truth. Did the powers granted to me by the stars call to other kinds of magic, like Tianna's, or what was in between the pages of this old book?

Only one way to find out.

Gingerly opening it, I leafed through the pages of the text, trying to make sense out of nonsense. I didn't know why I bothered with the book, I couldn't read the strange markings. Yet, the title was in English. It didn't make sense. Why title a book in one language, but have the script be in another? The book was so old, I found it hard to believe English was even a language when it was written.

Hours went by as I examined each page, staring at the intricate swirls, accents, and glyphs penned into the journal. I couldn't say why I'd spent the entire evening combing through the pages when I had no hope of deciphering the symbols, but something pushed me on, page after page. On the first floor, the clock struck ten, and I glanced up from the book, stretching my arms and neck.

The candle on top of the table flickered over the parchment, and the pot of tea Juniper had left for me hours ago had grown cold. I was about to call it a night, as I flipped one more page, when the Star of Persuasion pulsed with one vibrant glow of amber light. I stared at the stone that lay beside the book, wondering what had caused it to awake. The only time the star had ever shown any signs of life had been when I found the secret door, which in turn, led me into the tunnels and to the ancient manuscript.

Was it trying to tell me something?

My eyes swept the room, scanning for… I didn't know what. Trouble? A spirit? Tianna? I peered through the doorway that led into my sleeping chambers, but nothing stirred in the other room that I could see. So, what had caused the stone to react?

Another mystery to solve.

I returned my attention to the open page, and something about the markings there tickled the back of my mind. A tightness grew in my chest, my blood warming in a way that had the seed of magic within me awaking. What was happening? I stared harder at the scribbled marks. Were the letters wobbling? I blinked, and my heart thumped harder in my chest.

The marks weren't just blurry; they were shifting, reforming themselves.

My fingers clutched the sides of the table to keep them from trembling, while my mind tried to decide if this was good or bad. Probably bad, I concluded, but I couldn't make myself shut the book, or stop gaping at the glyphs that were now words—words I could read.

How was this possible?

My fingers ran over the text, unsure what I would feel when I touched the page, but the words were smooth on the paper. I did, however, detect a tingle of magic. The book read like a journal, with someone's notes jotted down for future reference.

"To restore what has been lost, place the object within a drawn conjuring circle. Do not break the circle until the words

of restoration have been completed. Any interruption will negate its ability to restore the power. For the spell to work, there must be a kernel of magic left in the item. Without this, the amulet can't be revived.

Magic requires a sacrifice. A few drops of blood from the spellcaster must be deposited inside the circle. The three symbols born from the language of the gods should then be traced inside the space, using the blood as ink. If the ritual is done correctly, the object's magic shall be replenished to its full potential. This spell works best under the moon."

I swallowed.

Could it be?

Had I found a way to restore the power of Tobias' star?

Did I want to restore its power? Was it vital to breaking the curse or killing the witch? Was that why I'd been led to the book, to this spell? Question after question whirled in my head while I stared at the text, reading the lines again and again.

It really was a spell to restore power to an object of magical devices—an amulet, like the Star of Persuasion. Yet, whether the ritual actually worked remained to be seen. I stared at the stone still sitting on the table under the candlelight, and my heart quickened as I waited for a sign or a signal that never came.

Was I doing this? Was I really going to perform a spell, in my bedroom, with no idea what I was about to unleash? I pressed the heels of my palms into my eyes and rubbed.

"What should I do?" I whispered to the empty room. No one answered. No spirit. No voice.

The halls outside my room were still. Nothing stirred. Was it even possible for me to perform the ritual? I wasn't a witch, but the book had said nothing about needing magic. Was I looking for loopholes because I was afraid it would work, or that it wouldn't work?

What did I have to lose? And with that thought, my mind was made up, so I stood to my feet.

I stepped into the hall in search of something to mark the floor with—chalk or a stone. The castle itself seemed to be sleeping. Down and down the stairs I went, my feet soundless and frigid on the tile floor. It didn't take me long to find something that worked—a charcoal stick in Issik's office—and I managed to make it back to my room undetected as if fate wanted me to cast this spell.

Back in my quarters, I pushed the table to the far corner of the room, making space to work. I gathered my dagger from the dresser, the book and the star, and sat on the floor. Setting the supplies carefully beside me, I picked up the charcoal stick and reread the spell slowly. I didn't want to make a single mistake, not even the smallest of infractions. Satisfied that the first step seemed simple enough, I took the charcoal stick and drew the best free-handed circle I could muster on the white floor. Hopefully, the gods didn't dock me points for my lack of artistic skills.

The hair on my arms rose as I placed the persuasion stone in the center of the conjuring area, and a phantom wind whirled through the room—sending the flame of the candle on top of the table sideways. My eyes quickly swept the space to make sure I was still alone, and a ghost or something else hadn't wandered in uninvited. Anything was possible now, with the secret door to the tunnels in the other room. I didn't trust any little noise or movement as insignificant, but the air died down, leaving me alone with the book and the star.

Taking a deep breath, I returned my eyes to the page, reading the next step. Blood. This part made me squirm. Why did it have to be blood? Couldn't magic demand a different price, like a lock of hair, or a sprinkle of holy water? Not that I knew where to get that either, but it was a lot less painful than cutting myself.

My palms grew damp with sweat as I clutched the dagger, preparing to pierce my own flesh. *You can do this. Just a quick prick and a few drops of blood. No big deal.*

Then why had ice frozen my veins? Why was my hand shaking as I brought the tip of the blade up to my finger? If I didn't get my shit together, I was going to end up cutting off a limb. I had to do it quickly, and before I lost my will. Closing my eyes, I applied pressure and sunk the end of the dagger into the pad of my finger.

At the first sting of the blade, a flash of Tianna's face materialized behind my eyes, as if she had been summoned out of the darkness. I froze, my entire body locking up, paralyzed with fear. The air in my lungs stopped as I waited for the next cut of her dagger across my skin, but the pain never came.

My eyes flew open, banishing her demon, but the wild fear lingered. *She's not here. She can't hurt me.* I chanted in my head until I wasn't trembling anymore.

Focusing on the star once more, a calming wave flowed through me. With a deep breath, I held my hand over the circle while blood welled on the tip of my finger, running down my arm. I pinched my index finger and thumb together, watching the light liquid drip, drip, drip into the conjuring area. The bright ruby red dots shone under the golden glow of the candlelight.

I returned my attention to the page, studying the three symbols I was to draw. This was the final step. Dipping the charcoal in my blood, I set forth to copy the first mark, careful not to disrupt the outlined circle. When I finished the first one, I leaned back, inspecting my craftsmanship. Satisfied that it was the best I could do, I drew the other two glyphs in a line just under where the star sat. The marks left soot and blood all over the white floors, and I idly wondered how I was going to explain to Issik that I'd ruined his mother's chambers.

Yet, the thought instantly vanished because I had bigger things to worry about. What had I done?

A ring of pure white light lit up the circle, beaming upward as if it were reaching for the heavens. Its energy pulsed like a force field propelled off the light, warning me not to touch it or risk being electrocuted—or something equally as horrible. Every single hair on my body responded to the sudden change in the atmosphere, including the hair on my head that now floated around my face.

The bricks, columns, and icicles that made up the castle rumbled at the outburst of magic from my room. My fingers grasped for the table leg on instinct, reaching for something to hold on to in the quake. An amber light suddenly flooded the room, emitting from the star, followed by a humming that grew louder with each second, until it was a chorus of a thousand angels singing.

Heart pounding, I scooted back on my butt, putting some space between the circle and myself just in case things went boom. My hand lifted to shield my eyes against the torrent of light, but it was hard to take my gaze off the stone. A thread... no, not a single thread, but three strands inside me tugged me toward the circle.

I gave in, unable to fight the demanding urge, and moved closer, keeping my eyes on the star.

"Claim me. Only you have the favor of the gods. Only you, keeper of stars, can wield my power..."

Then that blinding light erupted, leaving the stone in the center of the floor. The marks vanished along with the circle. The Star of Persuasion glittered a deep gold with flecks of orange.

"Claim me..." the stars insisted, as if they were not four stones, but one star.

My fingers lifted, stretching toward the stone, but I hesitated a mere breath away. If I touched the star, I would be accepting the power that came with it—the ability of persuasion. It wasn't something to be taken lightly. Already, my body had shown signs of distress from absorbing the other stars, but that could have also been a reaction to the magic I'd stolen from Tianna. Either way, it was a gamble.

Fuck it.

I exhaled and plucked the stone off the ground, waiting for sparks to fly, for the magic to happen. The Star of Persuasion didn't disappoint. Power crashed into me like nothing I'd felt before, so different from the calm of tranquility, the viper of poison, or the scorching heat of fire. Persuasion was smooth and warm, like swimming in liquid gold. It was unforgiving and compassionate in the same heartbeat. My body rippled and contorted as I rode the wave of magic coursing through my veins.

From far off in the castle, a roar sounded, but I barely

dwelled on what or who it could be. The other powers inside me all seemed to rejoice, swirling and mixing together like long-lost friends. With the side of my face illuminated by a small shaft of moonlight, and raw forces stirring in my essence, I never felt more alive than I did at that moment.

Or more frightened.

Thundering footsteps pounded outside my chambers moments before the door burst open. Four dragons loomed over me. My head lifted, with the Star of Persuasion still clutched in my fist.

"What the hell have you done now?" Jase demanded, his violet eyes piercing me with a glare that would have sent most girls running.

I released a long breath, hoping it would quiet the magic swimming in my blood. My hand lifted, and I opened my palm, revealing the glowing stone to the four dragons. Some things you had to see with your own eyes to believe.

As expected, utter silence fell over the room as their faces paled, and once the shock wore off, I had a lot to answer.

Jase pinched the bridge of his nose. "How?" was all he said, while the other descendants stared at me with their jaws still on the floor.

My arm fell back to my side. "I-I found a book." The response sounded lamer out loud than in my head, but I hadn't thought this far ahead. When I'd started this insane idea, I knew I would have to explain how I suddenly had the power of persuasion, but I naively thought I might have a day or two to digest the information myself. That was a fool's thinking when living with four magical dragons.

"A book?" Issik echoed as if I'd lost my mind. Perhaps I had with all this power inside of me.

"And you're just now telling us about it?" Jase rumbled. He towered over me in nothing but a pair of boxers, and it was then I noticed the others were all sparingly dressed. It was evident I had gotten them out of bed.

I sighed. My first night alone in weeks, and I'd still managed to get myself into a situation.

"Yes, but there's no need to get pissy with me. I fixed the damn stone. Isn't that what matters?" They were missing the point here. Sure, the castle had quaked for a minute, and I'd dabbled in a craft I didn't understand, but no one had died… yet. I guess the night wasn't over.

"I need to sit down." Zade pulled out one of the table's chairs that had been shoved in the corner and plopped onto it.

Jase bent down and picked up the Book of Stars. His brows lifted as he examined the title and thumbed through the pages, before his sharp eyes returned to mine. "Do you know what this is?"

"A book about the five dragon stars?" I phrased it as a question because, honestly, I wasn't sure what all the book contained.

Issik's intense eyes flipped from the book to me, a strange expression on his face. "It's written in the language of the gods. How did you read it?"

"Uh, I didn't." My fingers played with the stone in my hand, while I bumbled my way through an explanation. "What I mean is, I couldn't read it until tonight, when I stumbled upon a page with a spell. The letters rearranged themselves, and it became clear."

The four dragons shared a loaded look. "The letters moved?"

"Will you guys stop repeating everything I say? And

why do you all look so shocked? Doesn't stuff like this happen all the time here?" I'd had to deal with all kinds of strange and difficult to believe crap since I stepped foot in the Veil, while they were more than used to it. "I don't understand why you aren't acting like I just found the holy grail of dragon books."

Zade cleared his throat from his seat, his elbows propped on his knees. "So, let me get this straight. You found the book, and then decided to do an ancient ritual to revive the Star of Persuasion."

I blinked. "Yep. Pretty much."

Jase passed the book to Kieran, who scanned a few pages before handing it over to Issik.

"This," Issik said, holding the book in the air, "hasn't been seen in centuries. How did you even find it?" He handed the relic to Zade.

That was another story entirely. "So, it *is* like the holy grail of dragon books?"

Kieran's lips twitched, his green eyes bright in the dim room.

"Something like that," Zade mumbled as he flipped through the pages, occasionally gliding his fingers over the illustrations.

"How do you feel?" Jase asked, crouching down beside me.

My gut tightened at the question. "Like I just swallowed a pill of sunshine. My whole body is tingling."

Kieran gave me a mischievous look. "Persuasion, huh? This should be interesting."

"You think we should find Tobias?" Issik asked.

Jase shook his head. "Without his dragon, he has no connection to the star. I don't think he'd be much help.

Besides, he gave it to Olivia for a reason. Perhaps this was it."

Was he implying that Tobias might have known I'd find the book, and be able to restore the stone that had been entrusted to his family for centuries?

Kieran smoothed back his rumpled hair. "Who would have thought the book was hidden here this whole time? Issik, you never had an inkling?"

Issik stiffened. His cold eyes darted to where the book now laid on the table before they flicked back to me with an intensity that had icicles forming in the room. "Never. I'm very interested in how darling Olivia managed to find it. I've combed every inch of this castle multiple times in the last hundred years, and never once have I come across this book."

It was in that moment that I knew I could no longer keep the tunnels a secret. I told them about the door by the fireplace, the tunnels, and the treasure room where I'd found the book. I left out the part about the woman in white, but I mentioned the portal, confessing I had felt it rather than actually seen the opening into this realm, which was true. I'd only been told about the portal but had never seen it with my own eyes.

When I was done, Issik stepped closer. "Show me."

"Now?" I squeaked.

The stoic expression on his face made me squirm. "I get that you've had a long night, and are probably tired, but it would be a great help in securing our safety if you showed me the door. Growing up, I heard stories about the Westgard who built this castle—my great, great grandfather. He was said to have designed an escape route from the royal chambers. I spent my youth looking for the hidden doors."

Kieran snorted. "Leave it to our Olivia to find them in record time. It's what she is good at—finding the danger."

Wonderful. I rolled my eyes. "I'm not some world-renowned detective."

Zade's lips quirked to the side. "Don't underestimate yourself. From where we stand, you're that and so much more. You have no idea how special you really are."

Sighing, I placed a palm on the floor to boost myself up, when Kieran shot forward, taking my left wrist in his grasp. "You're hurt," he hissed, noticing the blood on my hand. He inspected the injury.

I'd completely forgotten about the prick to my finger. "It's just a small cut. The spell required my blood."

Four dragons scowled at me, a low rumble reverberating in the back of their throats like a pack of wolves. "The next time you get it in your head to do a spell, tell one of us so we can make sure you don't bleed out or something," Issik admonished.

I gave him a droll look. You'd think I'd cut off my hand. As usual, they were being over the top, but some small part of me was comforted by the fact that they cared so much. "I'll do my best." My reply earned me a few more growls of disapproval. No one was more surprised than I, when an answering growl came from the other room. "Tell me that was one of you," I blurted, jumping to my feet.

The descendants threw themselves in front of me, forming a first line of defense.

Cold sweat trickled down my spine. What were we dealing with? Was it Tianna? Had she sensed the spell?

117

Did she know I had the Star of Persuasion and had come to take it from me?

Over my dead body. I wasn't about to let her get her pointy nails on another stone. This one belonged to me and me alone.

Another vicious roar tore through the room, causing a dull throb in my temples—the beginnings of a headache. The night had started to wear on me, and the prospect of going up against Tianna right now filled me with an exorbitant amount of dread. My fingers slipped through Kieran's, with him being the closest, and his hand tightened around mine.

"How did it get past the wards?" I whispered, the words burning in my throat. Was this my doing? Had I unleashed something else with the spell? Or attracted it with the magic I'd used? Whatever it was, the thing sounded like a rabid beast with a nasty bite.

Issik bent down to pick up my discarded dagger on the floor. Bursting into a dragon wasn't practical in the small space, and they had all rushed to my room without a single weapon, an action I could see they were now regretting.

"These tunnels might not be protected by the wards, and if there really is a portal in them..."

Just as I'd feared. I'd been warned by Issik's mother not to linger in the tunnels.

"I think it's time you showed us where this hidden door is," Jase advised, moving slightly to let me lead the way into the bedroom.

Zade grabbed the candle from the table, lighting the path to the other room. The logs in the hearth were still warm, their orange and red embers glowing softly in the gray ash. I went up to the fireplace mantel, sensing the descendants watch my every movement, and spun the statue. The brick wall to the right of the hearth groaned as a slender gap broke from the bricks, revealing the outline of a door.

"She wasn't lying," Kieran murmured.

Swiftly, I stepped back from the door. "I'm not imaginative enough to make this shit up."

"I can't believe it's been here this whole time." With the dagger in his hand, Issik moved to press his shoulder against the door.

"What are you doing?" I hissed. My hand grasped Issik's arm while claws scraped down the bricks from the other side. The moment he opened the door, that thing was going to pounce.

His glittering eyes met mine over his shoulder. "It knows you're here, Little Warrior. We must dispatch it. If it got into the tunnels, then it can get out. We can't allow this thing to run around the Veil or bring others."

Disbelief swept through me. They were going to go up against a beast while half naked.

I knew he was right, but that didn't make releasing his arm any easier. As dragons or warriors, I still feared for their welfare. If anything happened to any one of them...

Issik shoved his shoulder into the bricks, and the door gave, swinging open to the darkness. I didn't dare breathe while something stirred in the shadows. Two crimson orbs gleamed out of the blackness. Zade waved the candle in front of the doorway, lighting up the stairwell I knew led downward and deep into the tunnels. The flame grew brighter, flaring with my distress.

The creature was something sprung from the devil's

nightmare. Horns wrapped around the sides of its three faces, falling in line with its bared canines. Rows of fangs poked out of its mouths as the beast let out another deafening roar. Its talons dragged over the floor with an awful shriek, and the ground trembled under its massive paw, slamming down in challenge. Animal to animal.

I blinked and blinked again, assuming my eyes couldn't focus in the dim light. Did it really have three heads?

Issik rolled his shoulders once before he plunged into the stark midnight of the passage, meeting the beast on the stairs. His name tore from my lips, but Jase and Kieran were there to stop me from mindlessly running through the doorway after him. I struggled against their arms, unable to suppress the instinct to help Issik, to protect him as they always guarded and shielded me.

Still, the width of the passageway wasn't big enough for both of us to fight the creature. I would only be in the way, so I stopped straining, and watched with my heart in my throat as Issik took on the three-headed monster.

The creature gave one snotty snort and barreled toward Issik. With his feet firmly planted, Issik held his stance. The blade became sheathed in ice under his frosty grasp. At the sound of jaws snapping in rapid succession, my blood froze in my veins. Issik lunged back, swinging the dagger through the air at one of the beast's throats. Blood the color of sticky tar spurted from the wound, covering Issik's arm, but whereas one head now hung limply to the side, the other two released a shriek of rage and sorrow that vibrated from one end of the castle to the other.

It rose up on its hind legs and thrust his claws at Issik's

chest, scoring his bare flesh with a bellow. Issik staggered backward into the room, but not before he pushed the dagger into the underbelly of the beast. Yet, the creature didn't fall. It stood on its back legs once more, advancing toward Issik like it was part man. Toward all of us.

What is this thing?

It tipped back its remaining two heads. Its craggy teeth dripped drool as it fixated on me with the anticipation of a kill, but to get to me, it would have to tear through four dragons. The bloodlust in its eyes was feral and not of this world. If given the opportunity, it would shred the descendants to pieces, bit by bit, enjoying each death, but the beast would save me for last. The intent of the animal was clear as it sized up our group.

I had to do something to stop it. The descendants needed an opening to cut off both heads, because I had a sinking suspicion that was the only way this creature from another world, a hellish world, would die. Issik gave no sign that his injury bothered him. His face tilted slightly to the side, the impenetrable mask of a warrior born to slay evil in any form.

My hands thrust out at my sides, power hurtling through me and singing in my blood. The stone in my grasp pulsed with fervor.

Kieran swore under his breath when he noticed my movement. "What are you doing?"

Shrugging him off, I squared my shoulders, and met the beast's eyes without flinching. "No," I seethed with a conviction that had the room buzzing with magic. "You won't hurt them."

"Have you lost your mind?" Kieran hissed between clenched teeth.

I couldn't break my concentration to answer him, or the beast would break free from the hold I now had on its mind. Apparently, I didn't need a manual to learn how to control someone or something, but I was going to give most of the credit to the stars. The combined abilities seemed to guide me, whispering what needed to be done, perhaps even informing me of the creature's weaknesses. Was that how I knew how to kill it? The stars had whispered it to me?

Something to ponder another time, when our lives weren't being threatened.

"She's using the power of persuasion," Jase whispered in astonishment, quickly followed by a command. "Zade, Issik, now! While the beast is still enthralled."

Zade stepped beside Issik, and together, the fire and ice dragons formed a wall of the hottest fire and the coldest ice—a combination that to any mortal would have been lethal—and some supernaturals as well. But this creature wasn't so easy to kill.

"We have to cut off its other heads," I informed them, while the wall of flaming ice kept the creature at bay for the time being.

"When did you become such an expert on killing beasts?" Jase shook his head. "Never mind, I don't want to know."

Issik held up my dagger. "Well, this will have to do." And with that, Issik lunged through the flames, the blade an extension of his brute strength. He brought his arm down with a force no mortal man would ever possess and cut through to the back of the beast's middle neck. It wasn't a clean beheading, but nearly. It took a second swipe to finish the job.

Thick, black blood coated the end of the dagger as Issik tossed the blade to Zade who caught it at the hilt, wrapping his fingers firmly around the leather binding. He turned to the last head, which snarled and snapped at him, waiting for any opening. Then he plunged the dagger into the top of the beast's head, through flesh and brain. The sound of the creature's cry was like a banshee's. Zade ripped out the knife, and used his next two blows to fully sever the head. It thudded to the floor, rolling toward Jase's feet, black blood streaking across the white tiles.

"I'm going to be sick," I muttered, my stomach rolling. That was something I desperately wished I could unsee. Kieran pulled me into his arms.

"I don't think it's safe for you to sleep here anymore," Issik wheezed, his breath labored from the exertion.

Hell, I wasn't sure I'd ever be able to sleep again.

I stood on a rooftop in the center of a city I never thought I'd lay eyes on again. Chicago. Skyscrapers jutted up all around me, tall and proud, crammed so close together it was as if they were stacked on top of each other.

Frowning into the evening wind gusting between the buildings, the air smelled of twilight and trash—a combination that wasn't pleasant, and one I didn't miss. A hint of rain hung in the air while nothing of interest happened below in the streets. No late-night partyers stumbling home. No nefarious deals happening in the back alleys. No taxis roaming the roads. The city and its twinkling lights were still.

And yet, I knew I wasn't alone.

My hand grasped onto the cool metal railing as I stared out over the city I had once loved, but now every memory was coated with pain. Why was I back in Chicago? More importantly, how did I get here? On top of a roof no less?

The building wasn't one I recognized, just another flat area with a makeshift garden, a few plastic lawn chairs, and a dodgy iron fence around the perimeter. The rooftop itself was in dire need of repairs, uneven and lifting at the corners. Water pooled in the pitted sections.

Once I had lived in a brick complex very similar to this one, and often hung out on the roof. It was where I'd snuck my first cigarette, and where I'd run to when I wanted to be alone or cry. The vast skyline always made my problems seem so small. Now, as I soaked up the view, I lamented that my problems couldn't be solved by a good cryfest or a long drag on a cigarette.

My life had changed, and there was no going back.

A blackbird squawked as it landed on the edge of the roof, drawing my eyes. The little critter shook out its ruffled feathers before tucking its wings to its sides. It watched me with an intensity that had a shiver running all the way to the base of my spine. Its claws clanked against the metal as the bird readjusted its grip, angling its head to the side.

Its silver eyes bore into mine, and I recognized the mocking look in them. The bird was laughing at me, and I could almost hear the haunting cackle that often invaded my dreams. It didn't matter what form or what world we were in, the thirst in those silver eyes was the same. What a bitch.

"Why am I here, Tianna?" I spat her name out like an old piece of gum, but kept my expression bored.

At that moment, a chill wind blew in from Lake Michigan, and with it, the blackbird lifted its wings, throwing back its head. Those wings became slender alabaster arms, the black feathers transforming into a flattering dress that hugged the curves of a woman. Strands of long red hair fell in waves over her bare shoulders, and in nothing but a few blinks, Tianna stood before me, her skin shining like moonlight.

"Olivia, my dear, such a beautiful night out in the city." She smiled in that unmerciful way of hers—wicked and villainous.

"I thought you would like a trip down memory lane, considering what day it is."

What the hell was she talking about? What was so important about today of all days? I didn't want to fall for another of her foul tricks, but my brain was still trying to work through what she was getting at with this parody. What day was it? In the Veil, dates hardly mattered, except for one. Summer solstice. It was less than a month away, which meant it was June.

My heart dropped into my stomach, and stayed there, twisting and churning as though a dagger had pierced it. Had it really been a year? June, my mind echoed. It was the month my mother had died.

Today was the one-year anniversary of her death.

I didn't want to know how Tianna acquired the knowledge. Having her be the one to remind me of the most tragic thing that had ever happened in my life, made me want to rip out her tongue with my bare hands. That was one way of silencing the witch.

"You didn't forget, did you?" She lifted a hand to her chest in mock surprise, the golden bracelets on her wrists clanging together. "I hate to impose on such a sentimental day, but I'm sure your mother would want you to honor her."

"You don't know anything about my mother," I yelled, the words punctuated with actual venom—a green mist of poison spewed from my mouth.

"Temper. Temper." She tsked her tongue, like I was a child to be scolded as she waved off the cloud of poison.

My fingers curled into fists, anger trembling through my body so violently, that it felt as if the ground was shaking with me. Did she want me to lose control? Was that why she taunted me, to judge how powerful I was?

"Your magic will do you no good here, seeing as this isn't

real. This is all created from you. I just plucked out a few memories, and viola, we have the city to ourselves. You have quite the eclectic memory bank."

"Get the hell out of my head," I growled, baring my teeth.

Her scarlet lips curved into something ancient and sinister, reminding me just how old and dangerous she was. "I guess we've gotten the pleasantries out of the way."

The tapping of her spiked heels against the roof echoed through the city, and my eyes followed her every movement. I wasn't buying the whole "I can't hurt you here" act. She was a witch. Nowhere was safe, not even my dreams, and this had to be that—a never-ending nightmare.

"You stole something that belonged to me, you little thief."

I moved away from the banister, positioning myself in a less vulnerable spot—not wanting to be shoved over the edge of the building. My eyes never left hers. "I guess that makes us even," I retorted.

She laughed, and my chest tightened. "Not quite. You owe me something in return." Her voice was low and threatening.

"And let me guess, you want the Star of Frost," I asked with more bravado than I felt.

Her silver eyes took on a whitish glow that would have been pretty, if not for what lurked behind the look. "The dragons' pet has a brain, which is more than I can say for all the other girls before you."

"I won't give it to you," I assured, certain of that fact. The wind whipping over my face was cool, but fire scorched my veins.

Tianna took a step closer to me, the black feathers on her skirt fluttering. "There is only one minor detail... I have your blood."

"What does that even mean?"

"You'll see, my dear. You'll see."

I didn't like surprises, especially from a witch. "You're positive I can't hurt you? Because I'd really like to test out my new abilities on someone, particularly a worthy adversary."

Darkness seemed to gather around her, swathing Tianna in an armor of shadows. A flicker of intrigue sparkled in her eyes. "I'm flattered, but our time has come to an end." How quickly that twinkle had turned into something wolfish. "You have five days to get me the Star of Frost. Five days before I storm the castle. Issik's ice wards won't be able to keep me out. And remember, dear, I'm always watching."

Her warning slithered through the air until it was crawling up my neck, whispering its threats in my ear.

My heart beat so violently that breathing nearly became impossible. Yet, through the panic, an idea emerged, and I thought this might be an opportune time to test the limitations of hurting her in my dream world. I knew I only had a few seconds and had to make them count. The magic answered my call, unfurling inside and waiting for my command, but I didn't give Tianna a chance to see what I was planning. Without warning, I lunged at the witch as the tips of my fingers lengthened into claws made of flames.

"Not if you can't see," I roared, scoring my nails over her eyes.

Blood slid down her beautiful face, trickling into her mouth as she screamed like a banshee. Fast as a viper, the witch struck out with her hand, cracking her palm against my cheek. I went flying across the rooftop, tumbling onto the ground. Pain erupted from my hip, and my cheek stung, but I shoved myself into a sitting position. The sharp metallic taste of blood pooled on my tongue, and I spat at the witch's feet.

I smiled, my teeth stained red. "Go to hell." I could feel the *witch's blood and flesh under my nails, and I hoped the wounds scarred, marring her beauty and taking her sight.*

Ruby red scratches ripped her skin open on both sides of her face, scorched by the fire. "You will pay. You will suffer. And those you love will die!" She transformed back into the crow and took to the black skies.

I awoke in a dark room. Whiffs of rain, garbage, and burnt flesh still lingered in my nose, mixing with the scent of Issik—cool, crisp, winter pine. The dying embers in the hearth provided little warmth in the room, and I pulled the covers up to my chin.

Fuck.

What had I done?

It was hard to tell myself it had only been a dream, when every single moment of the nightmare had felt so real, from the wind on my face to the city lights, and the blood...

The feeling of her bloodied skin under my fingernails was still present... *My lip.* I touched the corner of my mouth—where the witch had cut it with one of her many rings—and in the glow of moonlight, sticky blood smeared my fingers. Both hers and mine.

"Bitch," I muttered, wiping my hands clean. That lying whore. Couldn't be hurt my ass. Good. I hoped her scratches and burns stung, and she got to feel some of the agony she was so fond of delivering. With any luck, the damage would be permanent.

I struggled to believe that I had turned my fingers into sharp, flaming weapons, or that I'd had the nerve to attack her, knowing damn well she would retaliate. Was I a glutton for punishment? Or did I just not care anymore? Perhaps I was just beginning to understand and embrace who and what I was, and the power that was mine to control.

Issik stirred beside me, his light blue eyes glowing like the moon high in the cloud-shrouded sky. The white sheet clung around his waist—blanket hog—exposing four dark gouges on his chest that had my face paling... again.

The creature was dead, but it didn't lift the worry from my heart. More would be coming, and would continue to hunt me down until I found the Star of Frost. Five days Tianna had said, but I had my own agenda. I would find the damn stone, not because she had ordered me to, but because it was the only way to end this curse and the torment.

With gentle hands, I traced the lines on his skin, measuring the width with my own fingers. The marks were at least three times the size of my fingers, and the cuts went deeper than he had let on. They weren't clean scratches, but serrated and messy that would leave long-lasting scars... like mine.

The Ice Prince and I had both endured wounds of war, and it made me sick with rage.

"Are you planning on setting the sheets on fire?" Issik's voice sounded in the silence, heavy with sleep.

It took me a few steady breaths, to calm the sudden inferno that had risen up and blazed inside me. I hadn't even realized I'd summoned fire magic until Issik spoke, but now I could feel it roaring within me like a living thing, ready to come alive.

Silently, he watched me gain control of my abilities,

and rein in the fire burning off my skin in waves. His fingers gently caught mine and he slowly brought my hand to his lips, in a kiss of frost that cooled my flesh. Yet, my eyes were still on his chest.

"I'm fine. They'll heal," he whispered roughly.

My gaze lifted to his as I rolled onto my side to face him, but the sudden darkness that flashed in Issik's eyes had me instantly on alert. Was it Tianna? Had the witch already come to seek her retaliation for what I'd done? Had I truly harmed her? My body stiffened alongside his on the bed. "What is it? What's wrong?"

Issik continued to glare at me, a muscle at his jaw ticking. "You're bleeding." The pad of his thumb lifted to my split lip, and with a gentleness that defied the Ice Prince's demeanor, he rubbed at my bottom lip, inspecting the cut.

A rush of air expelled from my lungs. That was all? He had me ready to leap from the bed, magic once again tingling in my blood. "A gift, courtesy of Tianna," I informed him.

"How?" he demanded, wide awake and prepared to murder.

"How does she do anything? Dirty and with magic."

Clearly, Issik wasn't satisfied with my attempt to brush it off. He wouldn't let it go until he got answers.

A defeated sigh left me. "She invaded my dreams, but I'm not the only one waking up with a reminder of our encounter tonight."

He caught my drift, and by the scowl on his full lips, he wasn't pleased. A long silence followed. "What did you do?" he finally asked.

"I gave her a taste of her own medicine."

"Olivia." My name rumbled from deep within his chest.

With the memory still fresh, my face fell, and I lifted my hands to peer under my nails. "I don't even know how I did it."

"Did what?" he pressed, his patience balancing on a thin line.

"I tried to gouge her eyes out."

"You what?" His voice rose as he shot upright in the bed. "She could have killed you. Of all the reckless things you could have done..." He raked a hand through his blond hair.

I sat up after him. "It was a gamble, but I called her bluff. I want her to know that I won't quake in front of her. Not anymore."

Something akin to pride shone in his eyes, a grin tugging at the corners of his mouth. "You're something else, taking on a witch. I should wring your neck."

"I'd settle for a kiss instead." I batted my eyelashes at him in the nearly dark room.

He glanced down at me with a shameful look in his eyes that had a thrill dancing through me. "She's using your blood to keep tabs on you, to break into your mind, and God knows what else."

A comforting thought. "Probably," I agreed reluctantly. In hopes of steering the conversation away from the dream, I ran a hand over the lower half of his belly, feeling the muscles quiver at my touch.

"What did she want?" he asked, his eyes darkening.

"She..." I started to say, but then I remembered. Today was the anniversary of Mom's death, and it struck me like an arrow to the heart, leaving me paralyzed with gut-wrenching sadness. The wound in my chest opened, blooming until I couldn't control my breathing, or the panic from digging its claws into me.

Issik felt the sudden onslaught of sadness that barreled into me, as I gasped for air. "Olivia," he whispered my name, but I couldn't hear it over my ragged breathing. I only saw the word form on his lips.

Torn, I lost control of everything, of the room, my surroundings, my grip on reality, my powers, and most of all, of myself. It all spiraled swiftly away from me, as if I was back in that stagnant hospital room that smelled of sickness and hopelessness, and the doctor in his white lab coat was telling me Mom had passed on to a better place, one void of pain.

I had called bullshit then, yelling at the doctor, at the nurses who had rushed in to help. The screams and the thrashing had continued until there was a sting in my arm, followed by a welcomed blackness. For in the dark, there were no feelings, no hurt, no loneliness, just... nothing.

"Olivia," Issik called, more forcefully this time. His gentle fingers were under my chin, urging me to look at his face. "Just breathe," he encouraged, becoming a focal point for me. I conceded, working on slowing my breathing. "That's it, just breathe."

Regardless of my slowed breathing, the frenzy inside me wouldn't subside. I couldn't restrain the mounting power ready to wreak havoc. My wild gaze flew to Issik's, warning him of the storm about to hit. He needed to take cover, protect himself. I was on the edge. I had to get out of here, had to get air. Magic crackled in my veins, a combination of tranquility, poison, fire, and even persuasion.

Instantly, Issik seemed to understand. "Just hang on," he pleaded, but that was the thing, I couldn't. He jumped out of bed, flashing to the window at the far end of his bedroom, which was nearly as large as his mother's room —although hers was on the opposite side of the castle in a tower that went up multiple stories. The glass groaned as he lifted it to let in fresh air.

Before the crisp breeze could reach my scorched cheeks, unbridled magic ripped from me, on a sob that broke from my lips and exploded over the room. Fire licked the ceiling; poison curled over the floor in a pine green mist; tranquility swirled around me like a violet cloak of vapors, and persuasion's invisible force field blasted out of me, along with an echo of agony that rang over the castle, waking even the dead.

Swiftly lifting his arms, Issik threw out a shield of ice around himself, and if it weren't for his dragon speed, he would have been thwarted by one of those elements.

Kneeling on the center of the bed, I gawked in horror at the whirlwind of chaos I'd created. The release of both magic and emotion had purged my soul, leaving me raw and full of regret.

What have I done?

Using the last bit of strength inside me, I banished the powers of the stars, my hands falling slack at my sides. Tears stung my eyes with a mixture of guilt and sadness, but although the heaviness still pressed down on my chest, my breathing finally leveled.

Issik shattered the wall of ice, shards raining to the floor. "That was unexpected."

He was telling *me*. It wasn't every night I woke up and became a tornado of power.

The low fire in the hearth had extinguished, surrendering the room to complete darkness. Exhaustion weighed down on me as I curled myself into a ball. "I'm sorry. I'm so sorry," I repeated.

The mattress dipped with Issik's weight. His cool fingers brushed aside the damp hair plastered to my face. "You don't have anything to apologize for. Trust me, we've all lost control before," he assured me.

I couldn't look at him, so I kept my eyes averted, staring at the rumpled sheets. My gut was a tangle of twisted knots. "Still, I could have hurt you. If I had—"

One minute, I was wallowing in despair, and the next, Issik was kissing me. It was more a kiss of comfort than passion, but it made me feel alive, and I didn't know if I should be grateful or feel guiltier.

His fingers entwined into the mess of my blond locks, pulling me into his embrace. No other words were needed, not with Issik. He just understood what I needed and demanded nothing in return.

My little breakdown instilled in me a renewed sense of determination, to wipe Tianna from existence, and propelled me into action.

"Five days before I storm the castle..."

That had been her warning, and I wasn't about to test her limits.

Five days.

A lot could happen in one-hundred-and-twenty hours. This was the Veil, and nothing ever went according to plan.

So, I didn't have one concrete plan, but a loose one. Everything else was up to fate.

I plucked an apple from a bowl in the kitchen, and peeked into Issik's office. He and the other descendants were deeply engaged in a discussion about what had happened last night. Specifically, the elusive portal, Tianna invading my dreams, and the fact I could get hurt in them. Before roaming to the kitchen for a snack, I reminded them that I had also been able to injure the witch in return. We could use that to our advantage if the opportunity presented itself again.

That got shut down real quick by four overbearing, pain-in-my-ass dragons.

Didn't they see that they couldn't always protect me, not if we ever wanted a chance of breaking the curse? The stakes were much higher now, especially because I had omitted my looming deadline from my encounter with the witch.

The chime of a clock from the great hall rang through the castle, and I turned away from the den, taking a bite of the apple. Let them discuss portals and witches. I had one task—to find the Star of Frost.

That was exactly what I was going to do.

Today.

Before any of them noticed I'd been gone too long, I took the stairs to the fourth floor of the castle and hooked a right at the landing, toward the room that had been mine until last night.

God, had it really been less than twenty-four hours since I restored the Star of Persuasion? Time seemed to be in a weird loop of countless minutes sometimes, and then other times, hours flew by as if they were mere seconds. I couldn't get a grip on my days and nights.

The pressure was on, breathing down my neck like a shadowy beast about to devour me whole.

I fished the stone out of my pocket, holding it in my hand. "You better do your thing. I'm counting on you to find the last piece, your lost sister. Think you can handle that?" The star appeared to be in a helpful mood, the smooth angles glittering like gold in the sunlight. But that wasn't so unusual, the stones were known to pulse with life on their own. Except, what happened next was definitely not normal.

"Key of dragons..." An ethereal voice that was neither male nor female but something else entirely whispered in my ear.

The apple I held in my other hand dropped to the floor. It thudded on the ground with a crisp and juicy whack.

"Hello?" I called out, scanning the shadows for the source of the voice, but I already knew I'd find no one. It had come from within me, versus a person or spirit lurking around the corner.

"Your fate awaits you, and in it your future."

"Who are you? What do you know about my future?" I demanded, feeling like a fool.

"You are bound to this world, to us, in life, death, and beyond. We belong to you as much as you belong to us."

The fact that I hadn't started running and screaming yet, was a testament to how accustomed I'd become to bizarre things happening to me—including unexplained voices in my head. A shrink would have a heyday with me.

I bent down and picked up my bruised apple. "Are you the Stars of Dragons?"

"We are far more than stars. We are the spirits of gods long since forgotten. We are power, life, and death. We are you."

Oh man. That was a little too deep for me, a spiritual plane I wasn't ready to dissect, but I'd roll with it. "Great, then let's find the missing piece."

"She's close," the voice assured me, and I hoped it was one I could trust.

"Like in the castle?" I asked for clarity.

"Not precisely."

"Wonderful. You're about as much help as the women in white," I mumbled and continued to walk down the corridor.

Standing in front of the door leading into my old chambers, I stare at the handle as if it would bite me the moment I touched it. Perhaps it would. Nevertheless, every bone in my body was telling me the answers I needed lay beyond this door.

I should leave, or at the very least, grab one of the descendants to accompany me on this suicide quest I was hell-bent on pursuing. Yet, my fingers reached for the ornate iron handle as if an invisible force was guiding me.

"Yes. Yes. Yes," the stars purred.

My hands met an unforeseen resistance when I turned the handle. "Shit." I exhaled. Issik had locked the door—no doubt to deter me from doing something stupid… as I was now.

"Unlock it," the voice inside me commanded.

How? I wasn't a thief or a master locksmith. I had no skills at breaking and entering. However, I did have magic. Surely, no little lock could keep me out.

I went through a series of ideas based on my powers, looking for the best possible option. Finding the key was out of the question, even if I could *persuade* Issik to tell me where it was. The idea had merit and I could practice my new skill, but I shut it down as swiftly as it had entered my mind. Some lines weren't meant to be crossed, and taking away my dragons' free will wasn't something I would ever do.

Unless it was to save their life, but even then, it didn't feel right.

Only one solution seemed likely to work. I just hoped I didn't set the castle on fire. Controlled and contained. I could do this. Although it would be a shame to melt something so pretty.

My hand covered the lock, sending a stream of molten heat into the crevices of the iron. I gave it a minute before I tried the door again.

A satisfied smile curled my lips as the handle clicked and the door swung open. Thank the stars.

The air in the bedroom of the former queen of Iculon was twenty degrees colder than the rest of the castle. The room was still stunning with its billowing white curtains, gold accents, and the lovely canopy bed frame. My skin prickled from the cold as I walked farther into the bedroom, and toward the hearth. A draft blew in from under the secret door. I had been driven to this room, to the tunnels.

I placed my ear to the icy bricks, listening for any movement or sound, like a snarling beast with teeth sharp enough to rip the arms from my body. Only the howling of the winds beating against the castle could be heard. No wet panting. No razor-sharp claws scraping against stone. No witch cackling.

It was now or never. If I didn't open the door, I was going to lose my nerve, and run back down those stairs into the safety of the dragons. My fingers trembled as they reached for the statue, spinning her in a full circle. *You have nothing to fear. You're not helpless.*

"And you're not alone," the stars reminded me.

Right.

With my chin raised, I put my shoulder against the brick door that had revealed itself. This was the worst idea, especially since last night there had been a three-headed beast at the entrance, who had wanted to gut me, and probably eat me as its main course.

I glanced over at the bed, where I'd left the Book of Stars. *Go*, it seemed to say. *Go. And be quick.*

Pushy book of magic.

I put a foot over the threshold, peering down the stairwell of utter darkness—correction: utter doom, because that's what it felt like to me. The descendants were going to have my head, and if I didn't want them to stop me, I had to go. Now.

My other foot lifted.

"What are you doing?" a menacing voice thundered, making me squeal.

Shit. I spun, glaring at a golden dragon with mahogany hair as he leaned a shoulder on the doorframe. "Goddammit, Zade. I nearly tumbled down these stairs and broke my neck."

His expression didn't change. The faint amusement sparkling in his eyes never dulled. "I would have caught you."

I released a breath that became visible in the cold air. "*So* not the point," I mumbled, willing my heart to come out of my stomach, where it had dropped.

"You didn't answer my question, Little Gem."

"What does it look like I'm doing?" I retorted with a mega eye roll.

His gaze moved from my face to the pathway behind me. "It looks like you need a chaperone. There's no way you're going in there alone."

My mouth dropped open wide enough for a swarm of flies to choke me. "So, you won't try to stop me?"

He shrugged. "If whatever you think we'll find in the tunnels is important enough to risk your life for, then I can't stop you. Believe it or not, I trust you."

I wanted to assure him it was important, but truth be told, I wasn't sure myself that it was. Still, I had to go back down there. "Thank you, Zade, for not being a prick."

"I let Jase hold that title," he quipped with a chuckle.

A snort flared out my nostrils. No matter what sort of situation we were faced with, the descendants never missed a chance to jab at each other, but it was always in a brotherly way.

"You ready?" His head tipped toward the opening.

Summoning my fire, I sent a glowing ball of flames into the darkness to light our path. Its warmth chased away the eerie chill that had enveloped us.

"You're getting good at that."

My lips curved into a half smile while I shrugged. "I guess. It comes naturally now." Which was scary to admit.

Together, Zade and I hiked down the endless staircase and, at last, we reached the arched tunnel entrances. I opened my palm and extended my hand, counting on the Star of Persuasion to lead us in the right direction.

"You've done this before," Zade commented, watching me carefully as I guided the stone to each opening until it pulsed with a vibrant, glittering beat. His eyes were transfixed. "Unbelievable."

"You have no idea."

We traveled through the long-forgotten, winding tunnels, taking a different path than when I'd found the treasure room. Our footsteps echoed against the stone walls like we were walking in a tomb. Not a pleasant thought.

Ice infiltrated my body, spreading all the way to my bones. I swore even my nose hairs had frost on them. Why was it so cold? I let heat surge into my fingers and rubbed my hands up and down my arms.

"I assume we're tracking the star?" Zade guessed, moving closer to lend me his natural warmth.

I nodded. "It's somewhere in these tunnels."

His cinnamon-colored eyes were staring far ahead, scoping out what lay beyond the darkness. "Beats the bottom of a volcano."

I smiled at first, but then I remembered what had happened after I found the Star of Fire. I'd lost the damn thing to Tianna. The guilt still weighed me down, like the witch was pressing on my chest with the spike of her heel.

"I'm going to get it back," I assured. It was a vow I planned to uphold, and as I spoke the words, something inside me stirred, wrapping around my promise, as if the stars were magically binding me to the oath.

Under the flickering light of my hovering flame, the muscle along Zade's jaw thrummed. "Not if it means losing you. I'd rather have you than a family heirloom."

Though I appreciated the sentiment, it was more than a trinket passed down through the generations. So much more. And we both knew it.

I said nothing more about the Star of Fire, our feet shuffling along the dusty tunnel floor. Moisture thickened in the air, growing inch by inch the deeper we went. Icicles trickled down the stone walls, reflecting the orange ball of light. If it weren't for the consistent pulsing of the stone in my hand, I would have turned back, but I continued forward. Until Zade halted.

"Do you hear that?" he asked, his body stiffening beside me. The fiery dragon had been on high-alert mode since we stepped foot in the maze of damp and musty corridors.

Stilling, I listened, catching only the drip, drip, drip of water and… "It's the wind," I whispered, turning to face him.

He nodded, eyes bright. "But it's coming into the tunnels, not beating against them."

"So, there's an exit?" I theorized, trying to follow his line of thinking about why the direction of the wind mattered.

Zade moved in front of me. Nothing but a straight path lay before us. "It appears we're going to find out."

In no less than five minutes of walking, we came to an archway covered from floor to ceiling in cobwebs. It was thick and intricately weaved, like no spiderweb I'd ever seen before, and living in the city, I'd seen my fair share of hairy eight-legged critters. But this, this was something else entirely. This made my skin crawl.

"Something has been busy," Zade muttered, running a finger over the silken strands, and testing their durability.

The ball of fire hovered overhead, casting a soft glow on the threads of white. "Have I mentioned how much I hate creepy-crawly things?"

"So, I shouldn't ask how you feel about spiders big enough to eat humans?"

I shot him a dry look. He was joking. Right? "Only if you want me to start screaming like a little girl." The star in my palm suddenly gave a thrum of energy that vibrated through my hand. "Uh, Zade..." I held up the Star of Persuasion for him to see.

Flecks of fire sparkled in the center of his irises. "It seems we need to get through this mess."

Of course, we had to take the giant-spider route. "How certain are you that whatever made this trap is long gone or very dead?"

His features remained stoic. "Do you want me to lie to you?"

I waited a beat before replying. "Definitely."

"Stand back," he ordered, pulling out a sword strapped to his side—bigger and deadlier than my dagger. I hadn't even noticed him carrying it. A blast of fire shot through the air, glancing off his blade and straight into the network of webs. Zade's head whipped around, surprise in his expression as if he needed to make sure the source had been me.

I grinned, my fingers still tingling from the heat I'd hurled at the webs.

"That's one way of dealing with it." He nodded his head in a moment of teacher-to-student appreciation. "Well done, Little Gem. Perhaps I'd be safer behind you." He swept a hand through the air toward the now open passage, bowing his head slightly.

My eyes rolled, and I grabbed the front of his shirt, pulling him into the tunnel with me. "Come on, let's get this over with." I had a feeling we were on borrowed time as it was.

The pungent smell of ancient things and dust faded while we walked, turning crisp and fresh. We were close. My teeth chattered, the air had turned several degrees below freezing. Without the power of fire in my veins, my fingers would have fallen off already. The passage became lighter and lighter until the ball of flames was a source of heat instead of light. I quickened my pace, slipping twice on patches of ice coating the floor, but Zade was always right there to keep me on my feet.

Soon, we came upon a scalloped archway, with marks carved into the stone of the opening similar to the ones in the book.

I marveled at the sight that opened up on the other side of the arch. Zade and I stood on the edge of a cliff, and across a ravine of startling turquoise waters, was a frozen waterfall of glistening ice. It plunged into the still waters below, disappearing in its dark depths. Splashes of gold glimmered on the surface, reflecting the sun's glow. Icy trees clustered around the water's shore, dipping their heavy branches into the pond.

The arctic winds battered my hair, and I gawked, awestruck by the sheer beauty of the frozen waterfall. "What is this place?" I asked, wonder and delight lacing my words.

"That's a better question for Issik, but I have a feeling even he isn't aware of this place." Zade stood close beside me, in case a gust of wind took me over the edge. The landing was small, just big enough for the two of us to stand.

It didn't look as if anyone had been there in decades. In truth, it didn't look like it even belonged to this world but to somewhere the gods themselves dwelled. The soft lapping of water below drew my attention. "How is the water unfrozen?"

Zade's shoulders were tight under his dark tunic. His

body hadn't relaxed an inch since we'd stepped foot inside the secret tunnels, and now was no different. "It shouldn't be. Not here, not this close to the castle. It doesn't make sense."

Little did in the Veil.

The chilly wind pinkened the tip of my nose and cheeks, as I lifted my face to the sky. The star was warm in my hand, bursting with excited energy that beckoned me closer to the water. It called to the sparkling of power inside me.

I stepped forward, with only one thought running through my mind—find the star. A firm hand clutched my forearm, stopping me from tumbling right over the edge, and like I'd been splashed with cold water, I snapped out of it. Startled, my gaze met Zade's.

His gold-flecked eyes were bright with worry and tinged with anger he didn't try to hide. "Hey, what are you doing? I'm about to haul your ass back inside, star or no star."

My mind was reeling, and I was so confused. That sinking feeling of being on the brink of passing out crept up from some dark corner of my mind. "I—"

Then, I was falling down into the waiting world below.

Freezing air, swirling mists, and ice surrounded me as the drop shot my stomach up into my throat. My scream was smothered by the brisk wind hollering in my face. The rocky cliff, the frozen waterfall, and the dark trees were all a blur as I sped past, the kiss of winter embracing me.

I was going to die.

Where was Zade? Why hadn't he busted out as a

dragon and saved me with those majestic wings? Why couldn't I see him?

The fall was endless. I tumbled and tumbled through the eternal sky, until I thought that perhaps I'd stumbled into a portal, but then the plunge stopped, and I was suspended in nothingness.

"We have been waiting for you," a collection of voices announced.

Five of them. The mothers of dragons. The women in white.

They materialized from the gray mists, the ends of their white, tattered gowns dancing on a breeze I couldn't feel, only see.

"You brought me here?" I asked, attempting to work through what was happening.

"You are not safe here. Things not of this world linger. They are drawn to you and the power you possess."

"Because of the stars?" I asked, my feet oddly dangling underneath me.

"It is more than the stars." The eyes of the five women seemed to glow an omniscient white as they continued to speak as one. *"It is the kernel of magic and how it has transformed the power inside you. Nothing of this magnitude has been born, or felt, since the gods walked this earth."*

Oh shit.

"But the stone. It is here. I feel it. I can't leave without it," I tried to rationalize.

"She comes on wind and darkness. Her sight has been impaired, but it's not completely gone. She has other ways to find you."

Tianna.

"She will stop at nothing to find the final star. It is her last

hope. Desperation makes her deadly. But also weak. This is your advantage. You must protect the grimoire. It cannot fall into the wrong hands."

"You mean the Book of Stars?" I asked.

"It will be your key. Only you have the power to destroy the darkness that has consumed her soul. She is past redemption."

That was code for I had to kill the bitch. "How can I defeat her?" Even with my new abilities, I wasn't strong enough. She always had the upper hand.

"Your courage lies here, daughter." Together, they merged into one spirit, their five faces flickering over the one head. Their shared palm pressed to my heart. *"It is a rare gift. Trust in yourself. Let your heart guide you, and with it, you will find the answers you seek."*

I hated cryptic messages, even though this one gave me those feel-good vibes.

The one being spread out its arms. *"Now, open your eyes and truly see. Only then will you be able to find the final star."*

The five queens' forms shimmered, slowly fading away like the evening mist giving way to dawn.

What the hell had she meant by open my eyes? They were bloody open.

It was the last thought I had before the cursed falling resumed—that sense of dropping off the highest cliff in the Veil, with no dragon to save me.

But I worried for nothing because Zade was there, and he did catch me, in a way.

I blinked, coming to with Zade calling my name. His hands were firmly on my shoulders, holding me steady. His golden skin was as pale as I felt. A shaft of sunlight beaming through the trees illuminated the side of his face.

"Olivia." He exhaled my name on a loose breath, and

hauled me into his arms for a quick hug we both needed. Then he pulled back. "What the hell was that? Where did you go?"

Funny he should put it that way. My eyes glanced over the edge of the ravine, a brisk wind ruffling my hair. "I was here... but I wasn't."

His dark brown brows furrowed. "You're not making a lot of sense."

Still feeling unsteady on my feet, I moved closer to Zade on the uneven rock, seeking his strength. "It's complicated." Behind Zade, in the distance, a black dot stood out in the clear sky. It was miles away, but my blood chilled as I remembered the vision. "Zade," I rasped in a low warning. "We need to leave now. I don't have time to explain. You must trust me."

"Tianna?" he guessed.

"Yes, and something else. Something not of this world. We are not safe."

"What about the stone?"

The black dot seemed to grow wider, like a feral beast set on devouring the kingdom. "We have to leave this place before the witch finds us."

Glancing over the edge of the ravine, he slipped a hand to the small of my back. His fingers tensed at some unknown evil I couldn't see, but it caused caution to prickle my skin. "It might be too late," he murmured.

I caught the glow in the center of his eyes, and the claws that lengthened in place of his nails. Trouble had already found us.

"Whatever you do, don't make any sudden movements... or loud noises," he added, sizing up the threat still yet to make itself visible.

"Why?" I whispered.

Zade's eyes narrowed. "You don't want to know."

A distorted growl and gnashing teeth made my head whip toward the sound, turning my back on the tunnels. The good news: it wasn't a giant spider. The bad news: it was still huge, hairy, and ugly as sin. Not to mention the smell. I nearly gagged when the wind carried its stench to us.

The creature stalked out from the shadows, emerging from behind the frozen waterfall. Its white, milky eyes roamed over the waters, searching. Zade continued sizing it up, while the monster did the same to us as its claws clicked on the stone, moving closer. Its slitted nostrils flared, sniffing the air in our direction, and it was then I understood.

"The creature is blind," I whispered to Zade.

He nodded, having already come to that conclusion himself. "But that doesn't make it any less deadly. When the opening presents itself, I need you to run. Do you understand? You need to head straight to the stairs and into the castle. Issik's wards will protect you."

My hand squeezed his arm. "What are you going to do?"

"I'll be right behind you."

"Liar." If it was blind and had to rely on its other senses, surely we could use that to our advantage. "I can fight. Let me—"

"Olivia!" a voice bellowed from somewhere deep within the tunnels, a voice that eerily sounded like Issik's. The stone walls behind me shook with unrestrained fury, followed by a blast of ice that rippled out of the passage.

"So much for keeping quiet," I muttered, keeping my eyes pinned on the creature.

Right on cue, it threw back its hairy head, and answered with its own war cry—a challenge. The monster turned those milky eyes on me, as though it could see me, now filled with a ravenous desire to kill.

Zade flashed me his teeth. "Remind me to wring your neck when we get out of this mess." Rage transformed his features. "Run!" he snarled at me, right before jumping over the side of the cliff.

"Zade!" I screamed. Did he—? Had he—? The asshole had left me alone up here, away from harm, and had plunged off the cliff to battle the beast by himself. Always the valiant dragon, acting on instinct alone.

He had told me to run, but I found myself rooted in place, peering at the spot where he had jumped. Zade exploded into his dragon form before he reached the water. In the chaos of Zade's heroics, I'd lost track of the creature. *Where is it? Where the hell is it?* Then Zade disappeared into the coverage of the trees.

I sunk to my knees, crawling to the edge. My hands scraped over the rough rock, hard enough to make me wince, but it didn't matter. I had to see, had to know what was happening.

A roar that could only be dragon erupted. Zade shot upward, out of the trees, and the creature lunged from its hiding spot, slamming into Zade ten feet in the air. It sent the dragon whirling into the side of the cliff, rocks and pebbles showering into the water. Its ability to track Zade in the sky without seeing him was impressive.

Using its claws, the beast latched on to Zade's back. Zade rolled, flipping himself upside down to dislodge the beast, but its nails had dug deep into his dragon scales. The bastard had used himself as bait, giving me the chance to run to safety. Damn these selfless dragons. When were they going to let me stand and fight beside them? The time had come, whether they liked it or not.

Considering my options, I gnawed my lower lip. If I sent a ball of fire, tranquility, or poison, I could accidentally hit Zade, which would be epically bad for both of us. What should I do? Did I listen for once and run, even though every bone in my body begged me to stay and fight?

A black shadow in the sky distracted me, and the decision became clear. I'd forgotten about the black dot, which was now definitely a crow like the one I'd dreamt of last night. My eyes made out the wings as the bird glided through the sky, leaving me no choice but to run. I couldn't let Tianna find me and reveal how important this place was.

I jumped to my feet, frowning and glancing one last time at Zade and the creature. He would be fine. He was a freaking dragon, a fierce one at that. I had no reason to worry.

So, I turned and ran like hell.

And I kept running, letting the star in my hand guide me. It was as if it too understood the sheer importance of my safety, and putting as much distance as possible between the Star of Frost and myself. I didn't ease up my pace, not even when a high-pitched shriek pierced the air.

I slipped once, but was quick to regain my composure and forged ahead. More than once, I swore someone was following me, and the hair-raising feeling stayed with me as I twisted and zigzagged through the tunnels, the pounding of my feet slapping the stone. The Star of Persuasion was diligent in its guidance, warming and pulsing in my hand at each turn I needed to make. *Hurry. Hurry. Hurry,* it seemed to whisper in my ears.

"Olivia?"

At first, the sound of my name felt like a dream, distant and watery, but it rang out again and again, growing closer with each step. "Issik!" I called back and pushed my legs onward despite how badly they ached. My lungs were burning, and the maze of tunnels was endless.

Have I taken a wrong turn? Where is the staircase? Where is Issik?

Around the next bend, I finally saw him. He was there, rushing to me while loose pieces of his blond hair flew about his face as he ran. The Ice Prince was fast, reaching me in a few strides. He didn't give me a chance to say anything, but plucked me off my feet and hauled me back the way he'd come.

"Zade," I gasped, my breathing choppy and rough.

That made him pause as I'd hoped, and he set me upright, staring down at me with cold steel in his eyes. My legs felt as if they would collapse, but Issik's hands went under my elbows, preventing me from crumbling to the ground. "Take a deep breath," he ordered softly, and I obeyed. "Good," he said with a nod of approval. "What about Zade?"

"We were attacked," I managed to get out before stopping for another breath.

His irises crystallized. "Is he hurt?" he asked.

"I-I don't know."

"Shit." Issik gritted his teeth.

"Tell me you have more confidence in me than that, Little Gem."

That voice. That sweet, husky voice had the fire in my blood roaring.

I spun around, and there was Zade—naked, and looking worse for wear—but he was here... alive. He leaned a shoulder against the wall. Dirt and blood smeared across his chest and one side of his face.

My heart knocked against my chest, blooming with relief. "Zade, thank God." I slumped into Issik.

A lopsided grin curled his lips. "I told you I'd be right behind you."

He had. A sound part sob, part laugh bubbled out of me, and I took a moment to let my eyes examine him fully for any serious injuries behind the grime. He looked tired, but no real wounds that I could see in the dim corridor, other than a few minor cuts and scratches.

Zade stared back at me with mischief dancing in his weary eyes. "Stop. You're making me blush." His golden body appeared to glow in the dreary tunnels.

"He's fine," Issik snarled. "We need to get out of the tunnels."

"Agreed on all accounts," Zade replied, shoving off the stone wall and taking a step or two, but that was as far as he made it before he swayed.

Issik grumbled what sounded like a curse, before stalking toward Zade with me in tow. "Do you need me to carry you too?"

Zade slightly grinned, clearly exhausted. "If Olivia doesn't mind."

I rolled my eyes. How they could joke at a time like this was beside me.

Issik untangled his arm from around me and wiggled out of his sweatpants, leaving him in just his boxer briefs as he tossed them to Zade. "Put these on. I don't know how much longer my eyes can handle your nakedness."

Catching the pants, Zade tugged them over his hips with care. "You just want Olivia to stare at you instead of my... finer points."

A gruff noise of disgust escaped the back of Issik's throat as he gave Zade a shoulder to lean on. I slid away from Issik, allowing Zade space, and started to strut down the hall on my own. "Where are you going?" Issik barked.

"You can't possibly—" Yep. He could. Issik, one-handed, lifted me up against his other side, without breaking a sweat. I looped my hands behind his head and held on, too tired to fight him, or demand he put me down. Besides, I wasn't sure my legs would make the end of the journey. "You're impossible," I whispered in his ear. "But I love you." Then I rested my cheek against his.

"You and I are going to have a little talk later," Issik replied, his breath fluttering over my face, and sending a shiver of ice through my body.

The three of us hobbled up the never-ending staircase and into the sleeping chambers, plopping down on the lush, silk-covered bed. No one cared about the dirt or blood coating our bodies. I'd kill for a glass of water but couldn't move anytime soon.

Jase and Kieran found the three of us sprawled on the

bed, and staring at the ceiling a few minutes later. They had each taken a different path to hunt me down, after figuring out I'd gone into the tunnels.

"Is anyone going to tell us what the hell is going on?" Jase demanded, looking less than pleased at our comatose state.

"And what happened to Issik's pants?" Kieran added, wickedness sparkling in his vibrant green eyes.

I took one look at Zade and Issik and lost it. Laughter rolled out of me, flooding the room. I laughed and laughed until I was curled in a ball on the bed clutching my sides as the uncontrollable hysterics worked through me. I couldn't help myself. The humor of it all.

Jase and Kieran looked at each other, then to the three of us. "What did we say?" Kieran asked, his nose scrunching in the most adorable manner.

Jase folded his arms, his lips stretched in a thin line. "Perhaps they drugged her."

Kieran eyed me. "Is she drunk again? That would explain why she went off into the tunnels."

"She's not drunk," Issik growled.

Zade sat up, wincing. "Someone get Issik some damn pants."

Oh, my God. I couldn't breathe. It had been so long since I'd let loose like that, and heard the sound of my own laughter. The release felt uplifting and freeing. It cleansed me of the tension, fear, and anger binding my body and soul.

Issik waited until I gained control of myself before peppering Zade and me with questions. "What were you thinking going off on your own?" he directed at us both.

Kieran had fetched Issik another pair of sweats, and

tossed them to him on the bed. Issik slipped one leg in and then the other, standing long enough to pull them over his hips.

"You know damn well you would have done the same —*did*, if I recall correctly. Or did you forget the night you went into the volcano?" Zade pointed out to Issik's irritation.

Neither Issik nor Jase were having it. Kieran, on the other hand, stood in the corner smirking. That man thrived on the discord of others.

"That's beside the point," Jase retorted, in his best no-nonsense tone.

"She was already on her way into the tunnels when I found her. I couldn't let her go alone, not after we'd seen that creature. Plus, if there is a portal somewhere in that maze, she definitely needed protection." Zade wasn't the least bit remorseful.

"Tell me the blood soaking your shirt was worth it. What did you find?" Jase inquired of Issik, looming over the foot of the bed. His fingers gripped the iron post of the canopy's frame.

Crossing my legs on the mattress as I sat up, I turned the stone over in my hand. "The Star of Frost is definitely down there, but..."

Silence fell, a disturbing and horrifying quiet after the sounds of my laughter.

"There are other things that know it's there," I added.

"Tianna?" Kieran guessed, the gleam in his eyes quenched.

I shook my head, my eyes meeting Zade's. "I think it was guarding the star," I mumbled. That creature hadn't been there by coincidence.

Everyone's attention snapped in my direction, and Zade's brows came together as he mulled over the idea. "Guarding it? Could it be?"

"Makes sense," I replied, holding his stare. Bone-deep weariness had settled in, and my eyes were heavy. "Is it dead?"

Zade shook his head. "No, the bastard disappeared on me. It probably ran off to whatever hole it lives in, to lick its wounds."

My brows knotted and I blinked. "What do you mean *disappeared*?"

"Since when does a threat ever get away from the fire dragon?" Issik asked, picking up on the gist of what went down in the ravine.

A gust of warmth blazed from Zade as he sighed. "It wasn't one of my finer moments, but one minute it was clawing at me, and then it was gone."

Making a noise in the back of his throat, Jase strutted to the fireplace to stare at the ivory statue. "A creature that can cloak, or willowphase like a goblin? Interesting... interesting indeed."

I didn't find anything intriguing about the tidbit of knowledge. I found it frightening. "I need to get to the star it's protecting."

"We'll find a way," Issik promised, with ice-cold determination.

We didn't have a choice. *"Five days until I storm the castle..."* Tianna's warning breathed down my neck.

15

The moon shone high in the sky. A dark shadow moved through the night, creeping over a slice of the glowing orb. A lunar eclipse.

Perfect. Just perfect.

I took it as a sign. What better night than tonight to decipher a spellbook? There had to be something else inside the Book of Stars that could be useful.

Two days had gone by since my last venture into the tunnels, and in that time, we'd spent most of our hours in Issik's library, poring over the text inside the ancient grimoire. It was a slow process. Issik was not fluent in the language of the gods, making translation challenging, but it seemed important to learn about what was between the pages.

Now more than ever.

With each passing day, the window for breaking the curse became smaller and smaller. Then there was Tianna's threat. I had only forty-eight hours until I found out if she would make good on her promise.

We were so close, so close. I could almost taste the

sweetness of victory and freedom, could almost smell the air devoid of Tianna's dark magic.

And yet, the hurdles we faced seemed so much higher and steeper than any we had encountered.

I gazed one last time at the mist-shrouded mountains, and the shadowed moon before moving away from the window to join Issik on the couch. He had the book open on the table, which was littered with old parchments, dusty books, and empty cups of coffee and tea. We'd been at it for hours already, finding nothing of importance.

His hand rubbed over the back of his neck as I sat down beside him. He didn't tear his eyes away from the page he was trying to translate. From the furrowing of his brows, it wasn't going well.

Jase had a stack of books piled up on either side of his chair—one side to read from, and the other to discard those that proved useless. So many journals existed from the former kings, along with books of healing, agriculture, histories of the five kingdoms. Many of them had been brought here over the last two days from the other kingdoms—Jase's and Tobias's being the exception. Those were lost to us now.

In the front of the room, Zade stoked the fire—much to Issik's vexation—flanked by large frosted windows. I caught him a time or two scowling at Zade's back, while the flames leaped back to life under the fire dragon's gentle prodding. The dancing flames seemed to reach out toward Zade like a lover's hand.

While Issik and I worked on the Book of Stars, the others searched for whatever they could find on the crea- ture guarding the last star. It was decided that this particular beast, was an obstacle we were going to have to deal with in order to retrieve the final stone. Zade's answer to the problem had been simple, just storm the beast. He claimed there was no way the creature could best the four of them.

Five, I reminded myself. I was not going to sit idly by, not when I had the power to fight.

Zade's idea had merit if their abilities weren't dwindling, and their strength with it. Although none of them would admit it, I could see the change, and if I could tell, there was a good chance the enemy could as well.

I knew how much it grated on their instincts to sit around and read books, when every bone in their body demanded they take action, but sometimes smarts outwitted brute strength. We needed to know what we were getting in to before going gung ho.

While I had enjoyed the slower pace and lack of excitement over the last few days, I wondered if there was something more I should be doing than researching. People in the villages were scared and uncertain, their lives on the line. Jase's home was still encased in a spell, the people inside trapped, or worse, dead. And there were things that didn't belong in this world sneaking through the unguarded portal. Without their full powers, the descendants could do nothing to protect the Veil from the darkness that lived in other worlds. As long as the last ribbon of the curse was still tied around Issik, we were exposed to all sorts of dangers.

"Anything?" I asked, snuggling up closer to Issik on the couch to peer down at the book.

"Not unless you want to control demons, or summon a God," he replied, frustration punctuating his words.

Sucking on my bottom lip, I contemplated the options. "It might come in handy."

Issik and Jase snorted in unison.

"There has to be an easier way than this. My eyeballs are bleeding," Zade groaned.

I was inclined to agree. Days of poring over books was wearing on all of us, but on Issik the most. It was *his* star we needed to find, *his* freedom waiting to be claimed.

"Let me have a look. You need a break," I offered, nudging him to move over with my hip. It was like moving a glacier.

Issik dragged his gaze from the book to look at me. Shadows darkened the tender skin under his eyes. "I'm fine. Besides, how will you translate?"

We'd been through this every time I'd offered to help with the book, which he'd declined every time. "I have this, remember?" I said, holding up the Star of Persuasion. "It led me to a spell before, perhaps it can do it again."

The stone hadn't given a flicker of light or a beat of warmth since we'd left the tunnels. It was as if it too was drained, and needed time to recuperate its energy.

Issik's head dropped to the back of the couch, waves of coldness radiating from his skin. "It could all be for nothing, just wasted time. We don't even know what we're looking for."

"Maybe, but the stars do." I placed the stone on the table beside the book.

"A lot of good that thing has been," Issik grumbled, waving a hand at the amber star.

With my lips turned down, I stared at the star. "I think it's out of juice."

The flames licking over the charred logs warmed

Zade's pinched features. "Don't tell me we need to find a spell to rejuvenate it."

I shrugged.

"Not happening." Two words Issik was so fond of saying. Everything with Issik was *no*.

Instead, Jase was already plotting. He paced from one bookshelf to the other. "Olivia might be on to something."

Was I? Now, I was all ears and feeling smug as I leaned back on the couch, putting my feet up on the table. "Thank you."

Zade smiled as he stood up near the hearth, the fire-light glowing on his back.

"Don't leave us in suspense," Issik muttered, disrupting Jase's thought process.

Jase's finger tapped the spine of a book tucked into a shelf, his sable hair sliding forward. He was still working through whatever it was he was considering. Jase was the type of guy you didn't rush when he had something on his mind. "Perhaps having the stones together is the missing key."

I thought I was the missing key.

How many keys were there?

Issik's frown deepened, his head lifting off where it rested on the back of the couch. "Is that a good idea? We've always been warned about the power of the stars, and the need to keep them apart."

Zade shrugged after he had considered it. "What is the worst that could happen?"

Issik's chin rose a fraction, his ice blue eyes narrowing. "The world blows up."

"Your input is appreciated, as always." Jase scoffed.

Kieran strolled into the room with a giant bowl in his

arms and one of the housemaids trailing behind him with a tray of drinks. "I figured since we're pulling an all-nighter, we needed provisions." He placed the bowl of popcorn on the table, giving my braid a tug as he passed by to take a seat across from Issik and me in one of the deep, plush chairs. "So, what did I miss?"

Taking a handful of popcorn, I wrinkled my nose at him. My stomach rumbled at the smell of butter and salt. "They were arguing about the stars," I relayed to him, thumbing through the Book of Stars and shoving the popcorn into my mouth.

"Wait!" Issik blurted out, scaring me half to death. I nearly choked on a kernel of popcorn. He shoved the sleeves of his cream-colored shirt to his elbows. "Go back a page," he directed me with a wave of his hand.

Flipping the sheet of parchment over, I paused. "Here?"

He nodded, pulling the book closer to him, as his finger ran over the line of ancient runes. Everything about his demeanor changed while he read—from the concentration lining his forehead, to the twitching muscle along his jawline. His mouth set in a grim line, and the information suddenly made his face turn ashen. The brightness in his eyes faded and he cursed at the book.

"What's wrong?" I stared at the page of symbols, hoping it would translate itself in front of my eyes like the spell had done.

Issik's hand clutched the side of the table, ice spreading under his fingers and over the glossy surface on contact. The others stopped what they were doing to focus on him, sensing the sudden change in the room. All the heat was sucked out of the room, replaced with a frigid chill that had my breath clouding in front of me.

Finally, he swallowed and glanced up, his eyes fixating on me, but soon his attention went to the other descendants. "According to the book, if Olivia absorbs all five stars, the power will kill her," he addressed them as he spoke. Avoiding my gaze.

A grim silence descended upon us. Even the flickering flames in the hearth seemed to freeze, as if they too felt the magic of the book, the power of the words.

"It says a mortal's body isn't created to withstand the power of five gods, even if it is only a grain of their full ability," Issik whispered.

The air in my lungs vanished.

Jase angled his head to the side and studied the grimoire. "Are you sure?" He was questioning Issik's translation, needing to make sure he was confident. It was an error none of us could afford—me especially.

"Yes." Issik exhaled, a violent storm churning in his eyes.

Fuck.

Five stars. Not four.

I had doomed us all. The moment I'd restored the persuasion stone, I'd made finding the last star a death sentence for everyone, for the world. If I had never found the book, never performed that stupid spell, the Star of Frost would have only been the fourth. That was all I'd needed to break the curse.

What had I done?

Dust puffed up into the air when Issik slammed the book closed with a snap. His knuckles were white, and his eyes glittered like sapphires. "I forbid you from touching the Star of Frost. Do you understand me?"

My mind was whirling, and arguing with Issik was more than I could handle right now. "You're being unreasonable."

I understood it was a shock to us all, but did that mean we gave up? I wasn't ready to admit defeat. Not yet. No way. We'd come too far to say, "Screw it." Besides, Tianna wasn't going to just let this go. She had invested a hundred years into getting the power of the five stars, and sacrificed her sister to see the deed done. That was a kind of determination that shouldn't be ignored.

Jase gave me a sharp look. "This changes everything."

"Does it, though?" I countered, scooting to the edge of the couch.

"How can you say that? Do you want to die?" Zade growled, the words raw and angry. His eyes mirrored the flames clawing at the logs.

"What kind of question is that? Of course, I don't *want* to die, but not everything in life works out the way we want." My eyes flicked to each one of them. "I don't have a choice, or have you forgotten about the curse? More people will die if we sit around and do nothing. You will die!" I shouted, getting worked up.

A collective sigh went through the room. Issik stood up and stalked to the window, leaning his forehead against the cool glass. "If this book has a shred of truth to it, then the power of the five stars will kill you. I won't let that happen."

"We can't be sure," I argued.

Jase shook his head, and I knew they would gang up

on me with the sole purpose of keeping me safe. "We're not willing to risk your life on a gamble."

I glanced at each of the descendants, seeing a similar expression on each of their faces, but I wouldn't be intimidated by a pack of dragons. Future kings or not. If I didn't find the Star of Frost, they wouldn't be kings at all.

"The choice is mine," I declared. "And I choose to save the stars. Save this world. Save you." I didn't need a moment to think about it. My mind had been made up months ago. This was my fate. This was what I was brought here to do. If I was being honest with myself, the choice really had never been mine, but that didn't mean I was going to let anyone dictate what I did or didn't do.

Issik whirled around, pinning me with a look that would turn most people to ice. He was ready to argue. I could see it blazing like blue fire in the center of his eyes. "I can't live without you," he finally said, his voice just above a mere whisper, and the emotion behind his words was gut-wrenching.

"Issik," I murmured his name. They were going to make this difficult for me.

"We can't let you do this. We'll find another way," Kieran urged.

"Our time isn't up yet. Give us the opportunity to see if we can find more information," Jase reasoned, looking to pacify the situation with his levelheadedness.

I wanted to point out that, in nearly a hundred years, this was the closest they'd ever been to breaking the curse. There was no other way out. This was it.

Slowly, I blinked, understanding that nothing I said or did would help them understand. It was wasted energy I didn't have, not after the long nights we'd endured. I nodded, saying nothing.

This setback was devastating. We all felt it. Hope had been sucked from the air, leaving us suffocating in despair. I hated the emotion. Hated the way it crawled on my skin, making me feel stained with uselessness and failure. They might as well tattoo "loser" across my forehead. They meant well, but their love for me was clouding their judgment. In a way, part of me was overjoyed, thrilled even, by the depth of their feelings—to know they ran as deep as my own.

They didn't want to live without me.

But...

My eyes shifted to the window to see if the eclipse was complete. The red moon burned in the sky. An omen. A blood moon. If I believed in prophecies and fates, then this would be a sure sign of bloodshed to come.

Someone stood at the foot of my bed.

I could sense their presence. The feeling of being watched had the hairs on the back of my neck rising, yet when I opened my eyes, no one was there.

My heart beat wildly in my chest as I slowly sat up, surveying the room. Jase slept beside me, sprawled out on his belly across the bed, while his back rose with even breaths. Earlier that night a gloom had settled over the castle, and even the staff seemed to make themselves scarce, taking the chatter and livelihood with them. It had become a frozen tomb.

I wanted to defy the descendants, argue that they were

killing themselves for me, but their stubbornness made it impossible for them to see reason. Finding another way wasn't an option, not when we were so close, and out of time.

Sleep was a joke. I just tossed and turned, the sheets a tangled mess in the bed. Jase woke me a few times, whispering in my ear or pulling me into his arms. My body was so tired. I felt the exhaustion everywhere—in my bones, in my magic, and deep within my soul. But the dreams continued to plague me all through the night, the whispering of Tianna's voice.

And here I was again, awake in the middle of the night, that bead of magic inside me pulsing at the presence I was certain was in the room with me. The stars didn't seem to care about the consequences the book warned about. They, more than ever, encouraged me to complete what I'd started. The pull to the ravine in the tunnels nagged at me day and night. I didn't mention the internal struggle I was in with the power of the stones, knowing the descendants would only blame themselves. So, in silence, I suffered the demand they imposed on me, suffered the sleepless nights, suffered through the dark promises of pain and death Tianna vowed in my dreams.

But something was going to have to give.

And I was afraid that something would be me.

Would that really be such a bad thing?

It was what I wanted too. At least, I believed it was. At this point, it was difficult to decipher between my desires and what the stars wanted. The two had blurred together, muddying the lines of me and them. The separation between the two was almost nonexistent.

Perhaps I should give in.

I found it hard to resist, like a scratch I couldn't reach, and I just wanted the irritation to stop. I didn't want to fight anymore. I wanted to win, and to do that, I needed the five stars. We'd become one. My willpower was at its weakest when the dragons slept, like now, as if the stars or Tianna—perhaps both—knew the right time to wear me down, and when I was the least protected.

"Olivia..."

My eyes swung to the open door, toward the sound of my name. The women in white. Was it them calling me? They might have answers I desperately needed, a way to work around the death omen predicted by the Book of Stars. I refused to believe this was it. There had to be another way. There just had to be.

And who better to ask than the queens of the Veil?

Focusing on Jase, I checked to see if he had heard or felt anything. He was the lightest sleeper of the four dragons. Go figure. The tranquility dragon. The irony wasn't lost on me.

He was going to hate me in the morning, but I had little choice. This was something I had to do for all of us, and they *had* wanted to look for another way; this could give us that, even though I wasn't holding my breath for a miracle. I would accept the answers the women in white gave me, whether I liked them or not.

In sleep, Jase's ruggedly handsome face was peaceful. It was easy to see why I'd fallen so hard and fast for him. Any girl would. He possessed such a striking combination —obsidian hair, violet eyes, pronounced cheekbones, and his lush mouth parted slightly. I could gaze at him under the moonlight for hours. I burned the memory of his face in my mind, alongside Zade's, Kieran's, and Issik's.

Pressing my lips together, I blew Jase a kiss dosed with his own power. "Forgive me," I whispered as I swung my legs over the side of the bed. My toes touched the cold floor, and I slipped on a robe before sneaking out of Jase's room and into the dark hall.

The thought of igniting a fire in my palm crossed my mind, but I found the darkness wasn't a hindrance. In fact, I could navigate fairly well, my feet knowing where to go without being told. The silky cream material of the robe dragged behind me, making swishing sounds as I moved toward the staircase.

Lotuses didn't scent the halls like I'd grown accustomed to, roses did instead. I followed that scent to the main floor, and from there, into Issik's library. Without a sound, I pushed open the door and walked into the empty room, surprised to see the fire in the hearth still glowing. It had been hours since the five of us had been in this room. The aroma of roses was so strong that it almost choked me, turning the sweet scent into something potent and foul, like rotting flowers.

"The book," a woman's voice whispered. *"Open the book…"*

I didn't have to be told which one she was referring to, only one book mattered—the Book of Stars.

A slice of moonlight came through the window, falling upon the grimoire where it laid on Issik's desk, out in the open for anyone to see. Such a thing of magic and ancient secrets should be kept under lock and key, I thought, stroking the cover. The contrast was strange as I felt the buttery texture of the book under my fingers, and the condemnation of the words inside tumbled through my mind. Everything about it felt wrong, as if they weren't my fingers, and the thought hadn't been my own.

A purr of approval escaped me as magic zapped from the book to me, and a smile curved my lips. *"Hello, beautiful,* a voice that wasn't mine said. *What hole did you crawl out of? Let's see what sorts of sordid information you've been keeping hidden between these pages, shall we?*

My fingers turned the thin sheets of paper, my eyes scanning over text I'd nearly memorized at this point, but I was seeing it through a new set of eyes. This was wrong. How I was feeling, the smell of the room, the chaotic whirling of magic that rose up in my veins, it made my blood run cold, like there was nothing I could do to stop it.

The words on the parchment were no longer foreign as I mumbled the translations through my teeth, skimming over the pages. What was I looking for?

Answers.

Right. A way to retrieve the Star of Frost without killing myself and my soul.

Unfortunately, that wasn't what I found.

My finger paused on a page near the back of the book. A drawing of a five-pointed star was sketched under a paragraph, capturing my attention. *"Well, well, well. There you are,"* the voice in my head crooned in absolute delight.

Lifting my hand, I traced the lines, a smile tugging at my mouth. Excitement and victory bubbled in my stomach. My eyes devoured the spell written on the pages, reading it over and over again, until I could recite it word for word.

This feeling of being not quite in control of myself was familiar, and I was afraid of what it meant, afraid to realize the truth of what was happening to me. The women in white weren't guiding me, or waiting for me in the library. They were nowhere to be seen.

"Thank you, Olivia, dear. I'll see you soon."

As if someone had snapped their fingers in front of my face, waking me from a trance, I blinked. The memories of the last hour were hazy as I tried to recall why I was in the library and not in bed with Jase. I glanced down at the book, and it hit me like the crack of a whip across my back. My knees buckled.

Tianna.

The bitch had used me, used my blood. But that wasn't all. She could read the language of the gods.

I steadied myself on the desk, staring at the aged parchment. She had been after a spell, this spell. Again, I traced the lines of the five-pointed star, and my heart thundered in my chest so hard I thought it would burst through my ribs. A chill slithered down my spine. The runes that moments ago had been easy to read meant nothing to me now.

A strangled sob broke through my trembling lips. "Dear God, what have I done?"

16

Issik found me in his library moments later, curled into a ball on the floor and crying. "Olivia?" his soft voice called. The confusion and gentleness in his tone only made the tears come swifter and harder.

My shoulders shook with emotion. Had I condemned us all because I was weak? Because I struck a stupid bargain with the witch? A deal that had seemed like everything at the time, but now... now I wondered if I should have been stronger. Then, she wouldn't have been able to use me.

Tianna wouldn't have the spell.

His body dropped down beside me, his arms brushing up against mine as I hugged my knees to my chest. I felt his presence rather than seeing him, because my face was buried in the tops of my knees. Cool fingers brushed aside the curtain of hair around my face. "What's wrong? Tell me what happened. Why are you down here alone?"

In between those words, I heard the unspoken questions. *Why are you crying? What did you do now? Where the hell is Jase?*

Dejected, I couldn't bring myself to look at him, feeling as if I'd already lost everything, including the descendants I loved with all my heart, and there was nothing I could do about it. The tears kept flowing, and when it became clear I wasn't ready to talk, Issik scooped me off the floor, gathering me into his arms.

I didn't go willingly at first, not feeling like I deserved the consoling he so freely gave, but it only lasted a few seconds. I couldn't deny myself the comfort and solace of being in his arms. Even in this, I was weak.

I was broken.

Lost.

A failure.

I couldn't stop shaking, but Issik never let go. He continued to hold me, saying nothing. Sometimes the patience he exuded impressed me. Jase was often the calm one, but Issik had a quiet restraint that seemed endless.

My face buried into his neck, breathing in the crisp and wintery scent of his skin. Being close to him, and relying on his strength helped settle the raging storm of sadness inside me. I didn't understand how this bond between us worked, and I usually considered it to be one-sided, but perhaps they also could counter the emotions I was feeling.

Finally lifting my head, I dried my eyes with the back of my hand. "I didn't mean to wake you," I sniffled, knowing it had been my sorrow that had disturbed his slumber, prompting him to find me.

"My bond to you isn't a hindrance, or something you should apologize for. Your sadness was so deep it cut through me like a steel blade. I've never been so afraid. I-I thought…" He shoved a hand through his disheveled hair. "It doesn't matter now. You're okay?"

I wasn't. Not really. Yet, I nodded, biting my lip. I had to tell him what had happened, what I had done. "Tianna came to me."

Blue shards crackled in his eyes, like water freezing, and his body went hard and tight underneath me as if he was ready to leap to his feet. "Where is she?" he growled, murder in his eyes.

"She's gone. She got what she came for." His brow lifted, but I shook my head, reading the question there. "Not the star."

"How did she get past the wards?"

"Me," I stated flatly. It was the truth.

"I don't understand."

"She used my blood to control me."

He let loose a colorful string of words I didn't understand. They sounded ancient, foul, and beautiful in the way he let them roll off his tongue. "What was it she wanted if not the stone?"

My eyes shifted to the desk where the Book of Stars still sat open. "A spell," I answered, my voice cracking at the admission of what I'd been powerless to stop. It was embarrassing how easily she'd manipulated me. I had magic and more power than I knew how to wield, and yet, I hadn't been able to stand up to the witch, hadn't even realized I was being used until it was too late.

Issik's sharp gaze followed mine to the book. "She was able to read it?"

"Yes." If I closed my eyes, I could see the page as she read it, word for word, and the picture of the five-pointed star was inked into my memory like a tattoo.

He pushed to his feet, taking me with him and depositing me on the nearby couch before strutting back to his desk. "Is it this one?" he asked, holding up the open book for me to confirm.

I didn't want to look, to see the drawing on the page, but my eyes lifted. "I'm sorry. I'm so sorry," I said, feeling the pressure in my chest bearing down on me again.

Cool fingers framed my face, and I helplessly lifted my gaze to his, finding concern in his eyes. "There's nothing you could have done. Do you understand? This is not your fault. Besides, she can't perform this spell without all the stones."

That didn't stop the dread from tangling in my stomach. She had a plan.

And I had no idea what it was or how to stop it.

Every point in my body was numb—a hollow, cold silence that threatened to drown me. And when I did feel something, it bounced between guilt, grief, and anger until it ate me alive. Then the numbness returned, freezing my insides. It was like that for most of the following day. The descendants gave me the space I desired, but I couldn't decide which was better—the utter nothingness or the flood of emotions.

I was in some sort of free fall that never ended, and I didn't know how to stop it, how to pull myself out of the darkness.

How the hell could I find the last star and fight off a powerful witch when I couldn't leave the room?

Outside Kieran's windows, nothing but clear sky and

snowcapped mountains could be seen. The castle was so removed from everything and everyone. I sat in the corner by the window, gazing at the frozen kingdom.

A knock sounded at the door, and I forced myself to look toward it, tearing my focus from the glass. Kieran's expression was uncharacteristically solemn as he walked inside, spying me in the corner near the window.

He strode to the bed and sat down. "Did you eat today?"

"I'm not hungry."

"Do you want to talk about what happened?"

Thinking about it made my throat close up. "What's there to say?" My voice was flat, and my heart crumpled. How could I save them now? To do so would condemn us all.

Kieran's face was a grim mask, and it was a reminder of just one more thing I'd ruined—the twinkling in his emerald eyes. "Don't let her win. If you fall apart now, the bitch gets what she wants."

A faint ringing started in my ears. "Didn't she already?"

He rubbed his hands over his thighs. "We still have the stones, don't we?"

I shrugged. "She has me. I have the power she desires, and she means to take it from me, to use me as a sacrifice."

Kieran was on his feet and at my side in a flash, taking my hand as he sat down at the window seat with me. "We won't let that happen," he vowed.

Regardless of how dire and gray our situation currently was, Kieran still believed with that big heart of his that there was hope. I wished I could steal a sliver of that optimism for myself. I sighed. "Just promise me you will find a way to end her."

"We're not letting her take you from us."

Did any of us really have a choice? I pasted on as much of a smile as I could muster for his sake. He seemed to need it.

Kieran could see that I wanted to be alone and wasn't in the mood for conversation, but he was reluctant to leave. In the end, he slipped out of the room without me even knowing.

Once I was alone, I paced the floor for a good while, gnawing at my lip until it was swollen, red, and irritated. My slippers scuffed against the gleaming white tile, the silky material of my dress swishing with each turn I made.

Kieran's words echoed in my head. Had I just given up completely? Was I going to let her win? Was there anything I could do to stop it? Without the last stone, what could I do?

Something pecked at the back of my mind, something I was missing—a clue or a piece of the puzzle I needed to solve. It was there, within my reach, all I had to do was grab it, but the damn thing evaded me like a slippery devil.

There was a reason the women in white had led me to the book, and the book had pointed me to the revival spell. They wouldn't have doomed their own sons. The Star of Persuasion was my key to retrieving the final stone, but how?

It didn't matter. I had made up my mind.

Changing out of the flowy dress and into something more practical, I slipped into the hallway. I tiptoed down the hall, making the climb up the two flights of stairs, and from there, I let myself into my old room. This place was part of it. The tunnels, the ravine, the beast, it was all connected.

My mouth went dry as I paused in front of the hearth and stared at the statue.

Voices from behind the fireplace wall, deep within the secret tunnels, taunted me as an ancient wind blew in from the chimney, sending the dying embers dancing. I glowered at the door in front of me, a filthy string of curses reeling through my head.

I knew what I had to do.

I might very well be walking into a trap, but it mattered little to me anymore. This had to end, and sitting around doing nothing, sulking while waiting for Tianna to show her wicked face would drive me mad. If I was going to die, I wanted it to be on my terms.

With my dagger tucked into my boot, the stone in my hand, and the Book of Stars secured inside my red cloak, I returned to the tunnels, to where the Star of Frost had called to me the moment I stepped foot inside the secret door. I hurried through the dark passageways, going straight for the ravine. I had a plan—a loose, ill-thought-out plan, yet it was something.

An icy chill pricked my skin, and magic trembled at my fingertips the deeper I went, alerting me to the presence of others. "If you're watching me, see this," I muttered, flipping off the witch and her prying eyes.

I wanted her to find me, to see me. *Come get me.*

Approaching the ravine, a brisk breeze kissed my

cheeks, and I nearly stumbled on a rock. A curse slipped through my gritted teeth, my breath clouding in front of my face as I drew my cloak closer around my neck. I could smell the snow and the water trapped in the ice waterfall.

By the time I made it to the arched opening that led to the cliffs, I was out of breath. The star in my hand was throbbing with energy, sensing the nearness of its sister, the Star of Frost. I could relate, for I too felt it—that gleaming thrill in my blood. My powers seemed to rise up in unison.

One foot at a time, I stepped onto the jutting cliff, watching the frozen, cascading water, the ends of my cloak billowing behind me. *Where is your furry guardian?* I had to deal with the creature before I could even get close to the stone.

How the hell was I going to get down there? I peered over the edge, surveying the drop. I kicked a rock over the side and listened to hear how long it took to hit the bottom. This was one of those times it would have been damn convenient to have one of the descendants with me. They would arrive soon enough, but I needed to be down in the ravine when they did. It was imperative I retrieved the star before they came storming after me, or else everything we'd been through these last few months would be for nothing.

It shouldn't have been this easy, but perhaps it was because this was the path I was meant to take. The answer to my problem appeared in front of me.

Standing where just air had been a moment before, the creature bared its teeth, sending a low warning rumble out from its beefy chest. I could have sworn the ground under my feet trembled. Temperamental beast. I lifted my hands in the air and backed up a step or two, letting the creature know I meant no harm—not unless it tried to bite my head off, of course. Then shit would get ugly.

"Hey, there," I murmured. "Good, uh, boy." Assuming this thing had a gender.

With sharp and wary eyes the beast snorted, shooting some sticky substance through its nostrils onto the ground.

Gross.

"I'm not going to hurt you, but I do need your help." My hands might have been a tad shaky, but I managed to keep my voice even and calm.

The black fur on its neck raised as it tilted its head to the side, regarding me. It took a step closer, sniffing the air around me to take in my scent. A short barking sound came from the back of its throat, similar to a cough or a sneeze but much deeper and scarier.

"I hope that was a yes."

Taking a moment to collect myself, I gathered the power of persuasion. It swirled with the seed of Tianna's magic and settled in my throat. What I said next would be laced with an irresistible potency that not even the beast could deny… or so I hoped.

I cleared my throat, lowering my hands. "You're going to let me climb onto your back, and then you're going to take me to the stone you protect." I stared him dead in the eyes, letting my voice croon over him and watching as his eyes turned glassy. "Oh, and under no circumstances can you attack me," I added.

The beast didn't move a muscle, but continued to stare with that blank look. I took that as a sign and shuffled closer, sliding one foot and then the other as quietly as I could. A massive paw thudded on the ground in front of me, and the beast dipped its head to bow forward.

My arms shook as I reached for it. "I can't believe I'm doing this," I mumbled under my breath, moving with care toward the creature's back.

It remained surprisingly still while I hoisted myself onto its wiry hide, and used a fistful of long fur to grip onto tightly. The beast pranced under my weight, its feet fumbling on the cliff.

In a soothing gesture, I ran my hand along the side of its neck. "Easy," I purred. "Easy."

To my shock, it relaxed under the command of my voice, and I realized traces of power were still flowing through me.

With a shake of its head, followed by a snort, we were fully engulfed in a cool ripple of darkness, suddenly riding on the midnight breeze. It whisked us off the cliff, our surroundings disappearing. It took only seconds for the feeling of weightlessness to set in, and a different sort of freedom that couldn't be found in this world spread through me. It went beyond the boundaries and laws of mortals, witches, and even dragons. This creature was born from darkness itself.

From the blackness, the world materialized again. I was in a narrow ice cavern that seemed more like a bridge. On either side of the path, were two moonstone pillars that glowed like stars in twilight. One side of the bridge had a wall of ice so shiny, that I could see my reflection. The other had icicles of various shapes and sizes.

Fascinated by the sight, I swung my feet off the beast,

and hopped down to the slippery floor of frozen water. Everything in this place was made of sheer ice. Telling the creature to stay, I inched my way along the bridge, trailing a finger along the frozen wall. We were behind the waterfall, in a small alcove.

My head lifted upward, taking in the canopy of ice that twinkled over my head. The air was cold, cutting right through the warm material of my cloak. My gaze roamed the length of the ceiling and down the waterfall, causing my heart to leap in my chest.

Encrusted in the sheet of ice falling over the cliff was the Star of Frost. It emitted a pearly blue light, creating fractured rainbows that glinted off the frozen water all around it. I raised my hand, pressing my fingers to the glacial surface. The heat from my touch melted it slightly, leaving an imprint of my palm.

The beast whined at my side, as if it could sense what I was about to do.

"There is no other choice," I told it, my brows set.

Fire flooded inside me, but I hesitated. All I had to do was press down on the ice, and the flames would do the rest.

If it were only that easy.

This could very well be the end of me. So many regrets, so many wishes, so many things I longed to do with my life. And still, I had fallen in love not one, but four times. Who could say that? Some people chased love but never found their soulmate, and I had been blessed four times over.

This was for them. A gift for how cherished they made me feel, treasured, beautiful, and loved beyond belief. For the future of the most magical men in the world.

My vision blurred, and even then, I didn't realize I was crying until the warm tears slid down my cheeks. I dug my flaming fingers into the dense ice, melting it like a torch.

It took less than a minute to reach the stone.

Holy crap. I'd done it.

The last star was only inches away from my fingers. I just had to reach out and—

Abruptly, the beast bound to its feet, its low warning growl echoing around us, and I twisted my head to see what had raised its hackles. My dragons had arrived, looking none too pleased with me. The Star of Persuasion pulsed in my hand, as if urging me to return my attention to the Star of Frost, to seize it now, before the descendants could stop me.

I gave the stone a twirl in my palm, a reassurance that I wasn't going to let anything derail me from my plan.

"Olivia." Issik stepped forward, my name sounding like a curse on his lips. "What are you doing?"

"I think it's obvious," I answered softly.

Jase and Kieran eyed the beast that continued to stand between me and the descendants, issuing a ferocious rumble in warning.

"We talked about this, and agreed it was a bad idea," Issik sternly reminded.

"You did," I shot back. "Not me. I agreed to nothing."

"Olivia." This time it was Jase who called to me, his calmness radiating out of him like sonar waves, but I didn't hesitate.

My hand shot up, sending out a shield of fire to vaporize the mist of tranquility. "Nice try."

"Have you lost your mind?" Kieran whispered.

Slowly, I shook my head. "I wish I could claim insanity." Didn't they see this was the only way? Why was I the only one who understood? Well, and the stars.

"You weren't even going to say goodbye," Zade choked. Raw pain emanated from his cinnamon eyes.

I blinked back a fresh bout of tears. "I hate goodbyes," I sobbed.

"Then don't do it," Jase begged with a passion that speared my heart.

I glanced at him, picking up the panic in his violet eyes, but it didn't change what I must do. "How did you—?"

"I felt a spike of fear in our bond," Jase admitted, taking a step forward.

Of course. Their connection to my feelings was a thorn in my side, but it had saved my life on more than one occasion. I supposed I should have been grateful because it allowed me to get to this point. "You brought me here for this reason. Why won't you let me save you?"

"Unforeseen circumstances have unfurled. We never imagined this would be the sacrifice we'd have to make for freedom. I can't live like this... without you." His violet eyes pleaded with me.

"If I don't do this, the witch wins. Isn't that what you said?" I directed at Kieran.

The other descendants glared at him. "I did. But I didn't mean for you to kill yourself. I just couldn't stand to see you so... broken."

"Which is entirely our fault," Issik admitted.

"You promised to stand beside me. Always," I reminded, hurling Jase's words back in his face.

The hue of purple in his eyes fractured with pain as he too recalled that promise.

"Don't leave us. *Don't* do this," Issik whispered, and as my eyes found his fallen face, I didn't think he had ever begged anyone for anything... and probably wouldn't again.

It broke my heart, splintering it into a million jagged edges. "I love you. Can't you see how much I love you all?" I dared to meet their eyes, and wasn't surprised by the mixture of hurt, anguish, and betrayal that flared in them. I had lied to them, gone behind their backs. The anger was justified, but it wouldn't change what I had to do... not if it saved their lives. "There was never a choice. Not for me. I'm sorry."

"Olivia!" the four dragons bellowed.

I grabbed on to the Star of Frost.

Issik's face was set with feral rage as he whirled toward me, to stop me from touching the Star of Frost. "No!" he yelled.

Yet, nothing could stop what had already begun.

The energy burst through me, and my stomach churned as ice coated my tongue and teeth. My body shuddered from the assault of power transferring into me from the crystal in my grasp. I backed away from the waterfall, my eyes fixated on the stone. The air in my lungs felt like a blizzard. It took my breath away, making each inhale and exhale excruciating—like a thousand needles pricking my organs.

It hurt like hell.

I might have cried out and stumbled, for I heard someone call my name, but it was overrun by the surge of magic. Unforgiving and ancient, it encompassed every crevice of me. A flash of blinding light came from behind my eyes, and I knew the power of frost was mine.

A cloud of darkness misted my eyes. Black dots swirled like savage snowflakes, and I feared this was it, the end, just as the Book of Stars had predicted. Death was on the horizon, sucking me into its cold arms, pulling me into its never-ending depths. Oblivion was whispering in my ear, and I longed more than life itself to see, to touch, to tell the descendants I loved them one last time, but fate had other plans for me.

My time was up, and my only consolation was I had done it. I'd broken the curse.

Something inside cleaved through me, breaking my soul into five sections. Tranquility. Poison. Fire. Persuasion. And Frost. I threw my head back as a scream ripped from me, because what I was feeling, what was going on inside me, was too much for any one person to handle, and I crumbled to the ground.

I screamed again, my voice raw and shrill until I no longer recognized the sound coming out of me. It wasn't normal. It wasn't human.

Shadows wrapped around me like claws in its final sweet and grim embrace. Cold, numbing, and unforgiving, death pulled me into its depths until everything disappeared, even the sound of my heartbeats, and there was nothing left…

…

Then my screams began anew.

I became anew.

Something otherworldly. Something bewitching. Something divine.

The book had been right. I had died. But I'd also been reborn as something… different.

Not human. Not a witch. Not a dragon. Perhaps, somewhere in between.

The ice underneath my fallen body wasn't biting cold

as it should be. I told myself to breathe, to open my eyes—simple human actions we do without thinking—but suddenly, I found everything so profound. From the purity of the air, to the gentle caress of wind on my skin. My senses were heightened, making the world around me brand new.

I lifted my unblinking, sharpened eyes to the descendants, seeing them in a different light—clearer, defined, and vibrant. They were even more magnificent with these eyes. Given the luxury, I would have marveled at the sight of them for hours, but the expressions on their faces mirrored one another's as they stared at me. Terror and awe.

Beyond the shock, I could sense they felt a shift in their own abilities.

The curse was broken once and for all, and the release of it was written on Issik's face as he stared down at his hands, turning them over, and over again. Those invisible manacles were gone, which meant I had only seconds until the witch descended and the real fun began. She would know the moment the descendants were no longer held captive under her spell.

"Olivia?" Jase's voice was hesitant when he stepped toward me.

I held up a hand, warning him not to touch me—still unable to speak. What would I even say?

"We need to get her out of here. Now!" Zade thundered, shaking the ice walls with the boom of his voice alone.

Kieran's gaze went over his shoulder to the ravine outside the icy alcove. "I think it's too late."

The good news: I hadn't died yet.

The bad news: Tianna had come to collect what she considered hers.

Me.

A crow squawked, and the cavern went pitch black. From the darkness, Tianna rose as if she danced with shadows. Her laugh echoed over the ravine, followed by clapping. "Bravo. Bravo. What a performance. I don't think I've ever seen anything so heartfelt and tragic since Romeo and Juliet."

Instantly, I leaped to my feet, stumbling a bit. My equilibrium was off, thanks to this new body I hadn't had time to grow accustomed to yet. My fingers tightened on the two crystals, and I slipped them into my cloak for safekeeping. That was when I saw the glittering labyrinth of colors under my skin.

However, I didn't have time to examine or theorize what the fuck was happening to me. Tianna's sudden appearance sent a series of growls rippling through the dragons, but she dismissed their warning with a wave of her slim, alabaster hand, like they were nothing more than a pack of disobedient dogs. Scars raked over her eyes, a brand of my gift.

My eyes volleyed between Tianna and the descendants, finding I was the one who stood between the witch and the dragons.

"How does it feel to be free, boys? A long time coming, I'd say, but I didn't come to chat." She turned those heartless milky eyes toward me. "You've changed." She held up something in her hand, twisting it around. It was a black crystal, and at the center, something moved.

Holy hell.

It was an eye.

The witch had concocted a seeing stone to compensate for the loss of sight I had taken from her. The eye roamed over me from head to toe, taking in the network of swirls and whorls that covered my body, glowing like an iridescent rainbow. "Aren't you just intriguing? You get more fascinating each time we meet." A grin spread over her dark cherry lips. "I'm going to enjoy killing you."

A roar shook the stones, and the surrounding ice cracked as Issik burst into his dragon. The cavern groaned from the sheer mass of him, sending shards of lethal crystals raining down upon us. Shit was about to get real.

"Touch a hair on her head, and I'll paint the Veil with your blood," Jase threatened with a terrifying calmness that I'd never seen in his expression.

"You'll have to take each of us down to get to her," Kieran added, his claws lengthening over his fingers as he let a part of his dragon emerge.

"Olivia, give me your hand," Jase demanded, stretching out his fingers across the cavern.

It would have been so easy to lift my arm and intertwine my fingers with his, and yet, I hesitated.

Why?

Why the hell would I do that?

A sane person wouldn't have even given it a second thought, and here I was, caught between the witch, who had made my life hell, and the dragons, who had been my salvation.

I knew this war hadn't been won, not yet.

Tianna clicked her tongue at Jase. "You never could learn how to share." She spun on her heels, and that eerie eye in the stone gave me a mocking look.

Icy, glittering rage tingled through my blood. "You and I have unfinished business."

"You read my mind. Shall we?" She held out her black-tipped fingers.

I couldn't bring myself to look at the descendants, keeping my gaze centered on the witch. "I'm sorry," I told them, my voice hardly a whisper, right before I placed my hand in hers, leaving behind the silver-tipped mountains, the comfort of the castle, and above all else, my dragons.

"Olivia!" Four voices screamed.

Another roar ripped through the cavern, and Issik sent a blistering stream of ice in Tianna's direction, but her power had already engulfed us. A whirlwind of magic and darkness swathed me like a cloak. Large feathered wings of her crow form enveloped my body.

What had I done?

Shadows surrounded me as dark as a starless night, swallowing me whole. I might not have been able to see anything, but I could feel the witch's presence, her triumphant laugh echoing in my ears. My body was weightless as we soared through space, using the wind and night as an ally. There was no way out, no way to stop the journey I'd begun. I had no choice but to see it through to the end.

Tianna swept us from the hidden cavern in Iculon, to

the barren and unforgiving kingdom of the Nameless Lands. Although the shadows and wings had released their hold on me, my body remained unmoving, staring at the expansive, rough, and rugged land before me.

Storm clouds shrouded the sky above, and a mist hung low over the sandy ground, making it appear like grains of coal. Lightning speared the sky, and it was during the brief flash that I saw her. She was waiting under the shade of a gnarly, half-dead tree. The branches that were covered in leaves sagged toward the ground, as if they couldn't bear the weight.

My legs seemed to know what to do without me commanding them, or perhaps it was the witch leading me like a marionette doll. I stepped toward her, nausea and panic rising up inside me, but I forced my chin to lift while I moved forward.

"Welcome home, dearie," Tianna purred when I halted in front of her, a wicked grin on her crimson lips. "Let's catch up."

I pressed my nails into my palms, letting the pain center me, reminding me of what was real, for the witch was known for her tricks and illusions. "I'd love to, but we have a score to settle first."

"Oh." Her lips formed a pouty circle as if she was sincerely disappointed. She held a scepter in her hands, the creepy eye crystal was embedded into it, and the sight of her with the magical weapon produced a memory of the night she had betrayed the dragon kings. She had wielded a similar scepter then, except this one was made of bones—dragon bones.

Oh, my God.

They were Tobias's bones.

That bitch.

I was going to kill her. Or die trying.

Noticing that it caught my attention, she twirled the scepter, and its silver tip glinted in the moonlight. "Imagine what it would look like with five beautiful jewels. Dragon stones perhaps..."

The words were meant to taunt and enrage me. Well, she succeeded. A sudden upsurge of violence roared within me, and I would have struck the witch had it not been for her dark hold on my mind. Cool-tipped nails squeezed my free will into submission.

Tianna ran her fingers down the smooth length of the scepter, a predatory hunger in her sightless eyes. "Before you decide to be a hero, we have some unsettled business to attend to, and then, my dear, you and I can have that duel you crave."

"I'm not giving you anything," I spat. "It's too late. The curse is broken. The stars you so desire have been found. You lost." To prove my point and to let her know I wasn't afraid, I summoned a serpent from the mist. Long and sleek, its green scales gleamed, poison coursing through its fangs. The snake's forked tongue licked the air at her feet, coiling around her legs.

She chuckled, and the sound made me want to punch her in the throat. She extended her fingers toward the hissing snake as if she was going to stroke its triangular head. I narrowed my eyes, willing the beast to strike now, but the creature stared into Tianna's hypnotic eye. A moment later, the traitorous reptile wound itself up her slender arm, settling its head across her neck.

I silently cursed all the gods.

She had taken my magic and bent it to her will. If she

could do that with a simple smile or glare of her evil eye, I was doomed.

"Silly girl, that bit of magic you stole from me is just a speck of what runs through my veins. Besides, I don't care about the stones. It's the power I want—the power that is now inside you." Moving closer, she grabbed the end of my chin, holding my face steady and firm. "The stones are useless without their energy."

"Why didn't you just hunt down the stars yourself then? Why curse the descendants at all?"

"The gods are fickle beings. When they crafted the stars, and granted the five dragon kings a fraction of their own powers, they did so with caution and stipulations. You see, I am unable to touch them in their true form due to some ridiculous notion about my heart and soul. The stars only grant those who have pure intentions with their gifts."

My mind was reeling. When she had touched the Star of Fire, I'd received a piece of her magic. The star had extracted her power, giving it to me. But if she couldn't harness the stones' powers directly, then how did she plan to gain the power for herself? I was terrified to ask.

"You're a vessel," she answered, reading the question in my eyes. "I needed someone whom the gods deemed worthy to bestow their powers upon. It was the only way to release the magic from the stones themselves."

That still didn't explain why the hell the stars had chosen me. I was no one special, and I couldn't say that my heart and soul were pure. I'd done things in my life I wasn't proud of—stolen, cheated, lied. I was no freaking saint.

"How will you get the power from me?" I had an inkling it was going to involve pain. And blood.

She raised her arm with the snake still twined around it, and brought its head to her nose. Puckering her lips together, she breathed a puff of black smoke into its face, and the creature born from my power died at the hands of hers. "With magic, of course," she replied, dropping the limp creature to the ground.

"The spell. You mean to use the spell from the book to extract the power from inside me."

She tapped the end of my nose with the tip of her long, ebony nail. "I bet you were a straight-A student, weren't you?"

I snorted. Her question didn't deserve a response.

Her finger trailed up the seam of my cloak. "Since I can't physically touch the stars, I had to get creative. I needed a human that was pure of heart. That's where you came in, dearie."

Unblinking eyes stared at her with despise. Tianna had manipulated the descendants the whole time, in this elaborate scheme to grant herself the power of the gods.

My hand darted to the inside lining of my cloak, whipping out the dagger I had stashed there, and I held it to my own throat. "I'll die before I let you take it."

Tianna's scepter flung out towards me, magic tingeing the air. The dagger flew out of my hand and straight into my hers with nothing more than a twitch of her pinky. I could smell her anger. Her milky eyes darkened to the color of tar.

"I can't have that." She angled her head to the side. "Any other secret weapons stashed inside the cloak, or do I need to search you?"

She would enjoy humiliating me like that. "Go to hell," I seethed. "I'll never help you."

"That's why I have this." She produced a vial out of thin air, filled with a thick, crimson fluid. Blood. My blood. "A little insurance to make sure things go as planned."

Shit. Shit. Shit.

My face remained calm, even though a series of swear words went off in my head once again. The little vial gave me a nasty, sinking feeling in my gut. I had known from the moment I'd struck the bargain with Tianna for a vial of my blood that it was going to come back and bite me royally in the ass. Well, that moment had arrived, and it was devastating.

Reaching inside me, I let the power of ice coat my veins, preparing to hurl it at that stupid vial of blood. If I froze it and shattered the tube, she would have nothing to hold over my head, nothing to force me to succumb to her will.

It was imperative I destroy it.

My hand lifted, and I cast it out toward the witch, but sensing the power gathering within me, Tianna tipped back her head and took a swig from the glass tube. With a Cheshire grin, she licked her lips, sampling my blood like an exemplary wine. Before the arrow of ice could reach its mark, something inside me flipped. My magic sputtered and then was completely snuffed out, causing the arrow to halt mid-flight. It dropped to the ground, shattering into a hundred pieces.

A lump formed in my throat, and I attempted to swallow it. What the hell had I been thinking? Yes, I had broken the curse, but I had stupidly believed I could take her on alone—without my dragons—in some foolish dream of protecting them like they had done with me for months. I'd been prepared to die to save them, but this... this was a colossal fuck up. I had walked right into her sticky web, and was now trapped in a cocoon of her magic.

I tried to scream. To thrash. To fight. To summon every ounce of power within me.

Yet, it was useless. There was nothing I could do to stop the darkness of her magic from taking me prisoner. Again.

"Don't fight it, dearie. It only makes the connection between us more difficult, and by difficult, I mean painful... for you," she added with pleasure. "Your blood is now a part of me, which gives me a direct line to you. Clever, isn't it? Magic can be cunning if the wielder knows how to use it."

And she'd had decades to master her craft. I, on the other hand, had had just a few pathetic weeks, and my lack of skills showed in how easily she outmaneuvered me every step of the way.

"I'll give you points for trying. You never give up. There is something to be said for your tenacity. Now," she spun her pointer finger in a circle and sauntered closer to where I stood, rooted in place, "how about we get this ceremony started? We wouldn't want any... unexpected interruptions."

She pointed the scepter in her hands toward me, and my legs trembled as I fought against her command of my body. I gritted my teeth, sweat dripping down my forehead, but no matter how much I strained, my legs moved, carrying me across the barren plain a few paces.

"I promise this won't hurt... much." She laughed, and the sound made me want to shove her scepter up her ass. One of her pointed nails raked across my bicep, tearing through my flesh.

Hissing between my teeth, I dropped to my knees, the drawing from the book glowing in my head. The cut on my bicep was throbbing, blood trickling down my arm, but I ignored the pain.

"Your blood is the key..."

They were right. It had been the key. It had been what linked us together. What had led me to the stars. What Tianna used to keep tabs on me. And now it would be what destroyed us all. I had to find a way to turn the tide in my favor.

Tianna placed my dagger in my hand. "You'll need this."

My fingers closed around the familiar hilt and weight of the blade. I wanted to plunge the dagger into her black heart. I wanted it more than life itself, but that wasn't what Tianna willed. Biting down hard on my lip, I dipped the end of my blade into my cut. The deep red, lustrous blood became my ink to copy the five-pointed star from the book onto the sandy earth. Nevertheless, the symbol itself wasn't enough to complete the spell. I needed the five stars.

Two of the stars were on me. Tianna had one. But the other two were hidden in Viperus and Wakeland. Just how did Tianna mean to complete the spell without them?

My mind was whirling with possibilities even as I opened my palm and eyed the Star of Persuasion glowing a radiant, rich amber. Mine. This dragon stone belonged to me. The truth of that rang through my body, and the stone shimmered in response as if to say I belonged to it.

Was I really going to let the witch take it from me?

There had to be a way to stop this spell. I needed to find a loophole. And quickly.

I pressed the stone onto the top left point of the bloody star. On contact, the two lines extending to the next points lit up with a pure white that glittered like starlight.

Holy. Fucking. Shit.

Tianna's eyes lit up with wild hunger. "Yes," she murmured softly, her fingers gripping on to her scepter. "Now the next," she instructed me with a hint of impatience in her tone.

Unearthing the Star of Frost from my cloak, I nestled it into the bottom left point, the center of the stone lambent under the moonlight. Another white line emerged.

A tear slipped from my eye, falling down my face. I was relying on blind instinct, trusting the magic of the stars to reveal a Hail Mary that would put an end to this torment.

"The stones will only answer to you, as long as their power floods your veins. You must call them," she whispered in my ear. "Magic to magic."

I shook my head. "No," I uttered in a voice so weak, so quiet, that it sounded pitiful.

"You will," she demanded.

I had no choice. She had stripped that away from me.

Stretching out my right hand so that my palm faced toward Wakeland, I called forth the power of tranquility, summoning the crystal to come to me, to return and claim the magic that was rightfully its own. As she had stated, I was simply a vessel to keep the power safe until this moment.

I blinked. That was all it took for me to feel the thud of something in my open palm. My fingers closed around the cool, violet stone that reminded me so much of Jase's eyes, and I let loose a low breath. Placing it at the top point of the symbol, I watched as another line illuminated.

It was at that moment that I fully understood my role to the stars, and what I was fated to do.

My hand lifted to summon the Star of Poison when a deafening roar vibrated from the skies. The magnitude of its anger shook the ground under my knees.

Then another sounded. And another. My heart stopped.

Tianna's head whipped toward the dark clouds, the eye in her scepter searching for the first sign of the descendants. "Hurry," she hissed, waving the end of the scepter toward me.

Elation spiraled up through me. They had found me. Their presence gave me the courage of defiance, and only one thought echoed in my head. *I will break the spell that binds me. I will break the spell that binds me. I will break the spell that binds me.*

My hands fisted into the cool grains of black sand as I repeated the words over and over again, until there was nothing but truth in them. The three stones thrust into the earth, and the ones still in my blood intensified each time I recited the phrase.

I will break the spell that binds me.

Scorching heat blazed from the clouds, and a wind stirred with a cold that froze bones. Tianna cast out her scepter with her back to me, her feet planted on the ground, preparing to take on four full-fledged dragons. She was a powerful witch, and I didn't want to underestimate her evil nature. Her thirst for godly power made her a snake in the darkness.

Four dragons descended from the black skies. Daggers of lightning shot across the darkness that had wiped out all the stars and moonlight.

Magic simmered and brewed, becoming a song in my blood. I had to keep pushing against the binds of her energy that commanded me. I shoved, kicked, and pounded against that dark power holding me prisoner with my own abilities. Harder and harder I pushed.

My breath became a flame in my throat.

Ice wrapped around my heart.

My voice transformed into a chant of persuasion in my head.

Venom hissed through my veins.

And a steady calm of tranquility grounded me to the earth.

My attention returned to the spell, to the stars, and they purred in my presence. Like a rubber band snapping, the blood-hold Tianna had on me severed. It seemed the witch had limits after all.

It was my turn to take control.

Now was the time to strike while the witch was otherwise engaged with the descendants. I wasted no time in summoning the other stones. Lifting both hands in the air, one to the east and the other to the west, I invoked poison and fire, allowing their mystic energy to fuel my blood. Behind me, the flashes of magic, the snarling of teeth, and the vicious glory of battle raged, but I didn't dare look, didn't dare distract myself.

My right hand burned with fire and my left with fatal poison as the stones flew to me. An inhuman scream of madness reverberated around me, only to be overpowered by a blast of fire that sizzled and cracked in anger over my head. Yet, the ice in my blood kept the flames from burning the hair off my body.

I had to end this.

Positioning the Stars of Poison and Fire into their points according to the drawing, the last two lines lit up, completing the five-pointed star and leaving one last thing to do.

I swallowed, said a silent prayer to any gods that might be listening, and dragged my palm along the bleeding wound on my bicep. My bloody hand slammed onto the earth, fingers spreading wide into the center of the star.

"No!" Tianna bellowed, but it was too late.

The glowing white lines flowed like a river of starlight to the center where my fingers dug into the sand. The dragon stones hummed, and I listened, the voices of the gods whispering in my ears. Like a sleeping enchantress had woken up inside me, my head fell back to the sky. Pure, undiluted power pumped through my veins, a thousand times stronger than the stones had separately. Together, their power was endless.

I had done the one thing the descendants warned me about—combined the five stones into one.

At the center of the star, where my hand had been, laid a single luminous stone. Clear in color, like a diamond, it reflected a prism of tiny rainbows even in the weak moonlight. Picking it up, I prepared to unleash the storm raging within me.

"What have you done?" Tianna's angry voice hissed. "You little bitch."

Truth be told, I hadn't expected to make it this far, but that didn't mean I hadn't planned for what I must do next.

I stood, my movements fluid and graceful as I turned to face the witch, my magic building like ice lightning hitting a tsunami, that was burning with blue flames of poison. The magic inside me was a weapon. I was a weapon, like bullets firing in the night, arrows taut against a bow, a blade hissing with the winds. I was all of those things if I willed it.

Behind Tianna, my dragons formed a formidable wall of muscle and vengeance.

My chin lifted, knowing I must look like some alien, something not human, but I embraced it, welcoming the power granted to me by the stars—by the gods. "Your reign of terror ends today."

Although violence and anger rippled off her body, Tianna gave me a wry grin. "I hope you have the force to back up that threat, dear." She summoned the darkness to her in waves, pulling from the night surrounding us. She was greed and corruption, and from the pits of hell, her army was born. Creatures from other worlds and beasts made from smoke and evil magic lined up beside her. With a nod of her head, chaos erupted.

The descendants roared like dragon warriors, and set forth to destroy her soldiers while I took care of the queen witch. For good.

Tianna gave a silent command and then attacked. She flung out her scepter, hurling a dozen silver-tipped arrows at me, which undoubtedly were dipped in some sort of toxin.

Suddenly, time slowed in my eyes, and I became aware of each arrow slicing through the air toward all the vital parts of my body. My power rebuked her onslaught of filth. Lifting up my hand, I halted the fleet of arrows dead in the air, and swatted them away like nothing more than pesky flies.

Meeting her gaze head on, my lips curled into a wicked grin of my own. "Your magic is useless against me now."

Her face twisted with anguish. Those once beautiful eyes that were always full of hate, bitterness, and trickery showed an emotion I'd never seen on Tianna's face before —fear.

Around us, the descendants fought through ranks of Tianna's demon infantry. The sounds of searing flames, hissing poison, crackling ice, and the thuds of bodies hitting the ground in numb submission, surrounded me from all angles. Yet, I drowned out the noises of war and focused all that I had on the witch.

Sheer power trickled into my fingers, and I unleashed it. The white, fierce magic of the stars burst out of me. Through the blackness, my power shined, seeking out the infernal evil that lived inside the witch. The next second, chains of starlight wrapped around her tightly, binding her spells.

Tianna thrashed with a crazed rage against the shackles, but she couldn't break free from my dominant hold.

Confidently, I strutted forward across the dry land, my feet gliding over the earth until I was nose to nose with the witch. "How does it feel to have your abilities reduced to nothing?" I asked, kicking the scepter that had fallen to the ground.

With her arms pinned to her sides, her scarred eyes glared with malice, stinking of desperation. "You think you won? You think you bested me?"

I was going to incinerate the bitch.

"Yes." I bared my teeth. I was not a tool. Not a weapon to be wielded for warfare and glory. I rallied the last of my magic. "This is for my dragons. This is for Tobias..." I hissed into her ear. "This is for Corvina." And then, I detonated.

Tianna screamed.

I struck her again, my blood humming in approval. Her cries grew, cursing me to seven different hells, but I didn't waver in my retribution.

"And this," I whispered, letting the well of power surge up inside me until it was overflowing, "is for me." I couldn't tell where my body began, and the stars' energy ended. We were one. I blasted her one last time with everything I had left, destroying every drop of magic she had in her black blood.

The spell finished, and a ragged breath flew out of me as I swayed on my feet—my abilities and power depleted. Strong arms caught me before I fell, holding me against his solid, bare chest. Kieran. It was his scent of dewy woods that gave his identity away. "Is she—"

I shook my head. "She's mortal. Her magic is gone."

Tianna was on her knees. Her head hung so low that she could very well be dead. A curtain of glossy red hair covered her features, hiding them from my view. I watched as the strands of her vibrant hair withered, turning a dull gray.

She lifted her head, raising glittering eyes of horror to me. All her false beauty and youthfulness was gone, leaving behind a frail old woman. "How-how could you?" she croaked.

Feeling nothing but pity for the corrupt witch, I stared back at her. "For love," I replied softly. "Something you'll never understand."

The army of darkness had been vanquished the moment her magic was stripped from her. Now, the four descendants stood at my side in their human forms, and I leaned closer against Kieran, drawing on the strength of his arms.

We had done it.

The curse was broken.

The Veil was safe.

My work was done. And I could go home.

The thought stopped me. Where was home? What happened next? Would they ask me to choose between them? Would I bounce between kingdoms?

"*Claim it,*" a cluster of voices coaxed inside my head, almighty and familiar. The stars. They were a part of me, and I a part of them. "*You know what to do. It's your destiny. It has been since your birth, Olivia, Savior of Dragons.*"

I shook my head, unable to believe what the gods were suggesting.

"*This land, is yours for the taking. Claim it...*"

"Olivia?" Jase called, sensing something was going on inside me.

Were they suggesting what I thought? That I could claim the Nameless Lands? I could bring them to life? My eyes swept over the harsh and sorrowful kingdom, and my heart wept for what Tianna had done to it. "How?" I asked, ignoring the dragon for the moment.

"Give it a name."

"That's it?"

The descendants looked at me with concern and confusion. They were talking amongst themselves, but I pushed aside their voices, focusing on the stars.

"Your power, our power, will reshape this land. It will be yours to rule, to govern, to protect, to nurture, to cherish as long as your blood flows."

It couldn't be so simple, so normal, could it? Did I want a kingdom? I didn't know how to rule, how to be a queen. What they were proposing was insane. And yet, I couldn't deny I was tempted. A home. This place would be mine. No one could take it from me, or kick me out. It would be *mine*. My children's... and their children's.

What the hell. Wiggling out of Kieran's arms, I dropped to my knees.

"What is it? What is wrong?" Kieran asked.

"There's one more thing I must do," I replied, feeling the tether of their powers flicker inside me. I was so tired, but somehow, I found the strength to let magic dance in me once again. I threw my head back, letting loose the power of the gods within me. "Aylin!" I bellowed, thrusting the stone into the earth.

An electric pulse surged from my fingers to every crevice, every particle of sand, down to the deepest roots of the trees, to the very core of the Nameless Lands. Life flowed from the stone into the soil and beyond, the land taking what it needed to repair itself and start to heal.

The Nameless Lands weren't nameless anymore. Now, they had an identity. The kingdom of Aylin. We were united. Joined.

Beside me, the first bud of life rose from the dirt—a single blade of grass—and I grinned.

Four different voices echoed in my head, and as I shifted to face the descendants, I could sense the bond between us from ruler to ruler. Dear God, I was the ruler of a kingdom—my kingdom.

Zade's lips curled. "The queen of Aylin," he stated, testing the name on his lips. "I like it."

If any of them had an objection to what I'd done, I couldn't see it in their faces as I stared up at them, but there was someone who did—someone whom I had momentarily forgotten.

A war cry of rage and desolation shouted from behind me, and I spun to see Tianna charging toward me with my dagger gripped in her wrinkly hand.

Suddenly, Issik was in her path, his look was savage, unyielding, and vengeful. He struck out, grasping Tianna by the throat with one single hand. Without her powers, she was nothing. She was mortal.

His ice-tipped claws dug into her chest, freezing her black heart, and then he ripped it out of her. Tianna's inky blood sprayed over his forearm and bare chest, splattering over his glorious face.

Her shriek splintered throughout the Veil.

And then, a blissful silence ensued.

Issik crumbled her frozen heart in his fist. Shards of

ice rained over the ground, and as the pieces of her heart thawed, they shriveled. A gust of wind blew through, scattering the dead particles of her soul.

Her mouth was agape in a frozen, eternal scream of death. The last traces of her magic winked out, and with it, the dominion of bitterness and wickedness was annihilated.

The witch was dead. Truly. Forever. Dead.

Ironically, I found myself unsure of the future without a purpose or a task in front of me. What was I to do with my life now that Tianna was no longer a threat? The Veil was protected. The portal safeguarded. The descendants' powers were restored to their full glory.

And how magnificent they were.

Never had I thought they could be more impressive and majestic than they already were. I'd been wrong, and their kingdoms thrived under their rule. The four kings of the Veil.

Then there was me.

The keeper of stars.

The savior of the dragons.

The queen of Aylin.

Who would have ever thought a homeless girl from Chicago would become the queen of her own kingdom, and have power beyond her imagination? Certainly not me.

What would Mom think of my life? I'd like to think she'd be proud of me, of the woman I'd become, but perhaps not of the mess I'd created with my love life.

Four dragons. I had four gloriously gorgeous dragons who wanted me… at least I thought they did.

Gnawing on my lip, I stared out the window of my newly crafted castle of gold. It shimmered under the sun. The kingdom of Aylin had blossomed into a land of beauty over the last week. With its rolling green hills, fields of wildflowers, sparkling ponds, and flowering trees, it was truly a paradise. Every day I found something new to marvel.

Yet, there had been a hole in my heart these past few days. A part of my life was missing, and creating a home, building a castle, restoring the land had all been a distraction to what was really bothering me inside. The days and weeks after defeating Tianna had been a bustle of activity. The descendants had kingdoms to attend to, and people who depended on them, leaving me to tend to my home.

What was I supposed to do with a kingdom? Was I to be granted a crown of diamonds? Was I to just sit around all day, lounging in the gardens and eating fruit from the trees? Tobias had visited me once to thank me for bringing life back into the land that had once been his. He refused my offer to stay, informing me his days in this world were coming to an end and not to cry for him, regardless of the tears that had fallen down my cheeks.

With a heavy sigh, I turned away from the window and wandered to the fountain that sat in the middle of the foyer. Compared to the descendants' homes, mine was modest, but I didn't need or want a large home to get lost in. The castle was built, after all, by my own magic and imagination, a weird concept to wrap my head around, but I loved being surrounded by things that were mine.

And still, I was lonely.

Other than the occasional visits from the dead queens of the Veil, my castle was quiet. The women in white seemed to know when I needed company or guidance, as I did now. I had a feeling they would be with me always, queen to queen. We shared a bond.

As though I had summoned them, the five of them rose from the sparkling basin of the fountain. Their forms were not entirely solid, but more real now that Tianna was gone. *"Why do you look so sad, daughter?"* Eira asked, Issik's mother.

Roseria looked at me with concern in her warm brown eyes, much like her son Zade's. *"Is your new home not to your liking?"*

Were they kidding? It was everything and more than I could ever need. It had literally been born from my dreams, my wishes, and my desires. Magic was a marvelous thing, though I still had so much to learn about my newfound abilities. They weren't to be taken lightly. I never wanted to let the power I had corrupt me, so I needed to make sure I stayed grounded.

The material of my white dress swooshed against my legs as I moved to sit on the edge of the stone basin, the trickling water filling the room with a soothing sound. "I love my home. I love my kingdom. There is nothing more I could hope for."

"Nothing?" Wisteria, Jase's mother, asked with a single raised brow that reminded me eerily of her son.

Her tone had my eyes narrowing. "What are you implying?" It wasn't lost on me how unique and possibly odd some might find my situation—the fact that I frequently held conversations with the ghosts of dead queens.

"Perhaps you should seek them out, if they are too stubborn to come to you," Kelaya suggested, the queen of Viperus. Since these almost daily chats had started, I had learned a great deal about the mothers of my dragons, including their names. They appeared to be less bound by the laws of the world since the curse had been lifted.

My nose wrinkled. "Why would I do that?"

Adara sighed. She was Tobias's mother. *"I'll never understand young love. If you want something, you need to take it."*

"So, you're suggesting I just stroll into their kingdoms and kidnap your sons?"

A series of laughs echoed throughout the foyer, so light and girly for five ghosts who were so wise and dignified. *"You know that was not what I was suggesting,"* Adara replied, a smile still upon her lips.

"What if they don't want me?" *What if they make me choose?* I silently added. I couldn't possibly pick just one. I couldn't. The thought made me sick. And they deserved a queen who would stand beside them, give them children, and love them wholly. I couldn't do that, not if it meant I had to pick between the four of them.

Wisteria clucked her tongue, and I felt a phantom touch against my cheek as she brushed aside a strand of loose hair. *"You have nothing to fear. In your heart, you know what you must do. It is the only way you will ever find genuine happiness."*

My fingers played with the star of the gods in my hand.

~

The great thing about being a ruler in the Veil was I had a direct connection to the descendants, which came in handy when phones weren't a thing. After spending all night dwelling on what the women in white had said, I finally came to the decision that we needed to have a talk, and I was desperate to see them.

It had been too long.

I summoned the dragons to Aylin. Since I didn't have wings, and hadn't quite figured out how to willowphase, I was more or less stuck at home. It was driving me bananas.

Pacing the garden from one hedge to the other, I soaked up the sun as I continued to stare into the cloudless sky, searching for any sign of my dragons. They were still my dragons… I hoped.

Beating wings in the distance alerted me that they had arrived, and the sound had my blood racing. Seconds later, four dark specks appeared at various points in the sky. Zade and Issik's kingdoms bordered mine to the north and east.

Nerves and excitement spiraled through me, and I thought I might be sick. That would make one hell of a reunion. My fingers turned the stone in my hand as I fought for patience, and to keep from throwing up. The star of the gods had become a source of comfort, and I often found myself reaching for it in the long nights alone.

Issik was the first to touch down, his massive dragon feet landing with an icy thud in the courtyard, which was designed large enough for dragon landings. My feet flew over the cobblestone pathway, racing to the patch of grass in time to see him wiggle the pants over his hips, although he didn't bother with a shirt. I had a stack of clothes waiting on the edge of the gardens for such occasions, when the descendants showed up in dragon form.

A smile came to his lips as his eyes found mine just as I reached him. His cool breeze kissed my cheeks, smelling of winter's first snowfall. "Hey, Little Warrior," Issik greeted in that deep voice and pulled me into his arms. His lips were on mine a moment later, drinking from my mouth like a man dying of thirst.

I barely had time to catch my breath before I was spun around to face Zade, who had arrived moments after Issik. Molten heat engulfed me. "Little Gem," he murmured against my lips, chasing the cold from Issik's kiss away.

Next was Kieran. He didn't bother with clothes, coming straight to where I was being mauled by Issik and Zade. He flicked the tip of my nose before planting a quick kiss of greeting on my lips, causing my pulse to hammer. "It's been too long, Blondie."

I couldn't agree more. "I missed you too," I agreed with the biggest grin on my face.

Picking me up off my feet, Kieran spun me. While the world was blurring around me, I sensed Jase, his unmistakable tranquility. When my feet touched the ground, I didn't wait for the dizziness to pass before launching myself into his arms, welcoming the blissful calm that radiated from his skin. I drew in his scent like clean air.

Jase rained kisses over my face. "Olivia," he sighed. My arms went around his waist, and I held on tight. He was content to keep me there for as long as I wanted, neither of us pulling away, not until three males cleared their throats.

They were here. All of them. And my heart had never felt so full, so complete. The gleaming, golden castle was at my back, but their eyes were all on me. A thrill made its way through my veins, making me realize how much I wanted them in my daily life.

"Love what you've done with the place," Kieran offered with a lopsided grin.

I beamed. "It's home."

"I can't tell you how happy we are that you've chosen to stay," Jase confessed, looping a free hand around my waist, and walking with me toward the palace.

The others fell in step alongside us. "Why Aylin?" Issik asked, surveying the grounds.

"It was my mother's name. It means paradise, and that is exactly what I want this place to be. A reminder of her and of all that is good in my life."

"It's beautiful," Kieran agreed with a wink.

An awkward moment followed with the pleasantries out of the way. Zade offered me a wicked grin that was all dragon. "We've tracked down and hunted most of the creatures that managed to slip in through the portal these last few months."

"You've been busy," I admitted. While I'd been lounging around in paradise, rearranging all the furniture they had sent my way, and sulking, they'd been out making sure the Veil was once again a safe place. Why hadn't they asked me to help? I was more than capable of taking down the bad guys now that I was... hell, I didn't know what I was, but I had enough power to protect this world.

Violet glittering eyes swept over my face. "Have you settled in okay?" Jase asked.

I nodded, wondering how weird it would be if I just stared at them for hours.

"But..." Issik prompted, the faint smile in his eyes fading as he sensed my hesitation and the loneliness I tried to hide.

Having the four of them here with me again, being in their presence, I wasn't sure I could let them go this time. I shrugged in an attempt to keep things lighthearted and protect my heart. The fear of rejection, of no longer being wanted was making me feel vulnerable. I took a deep breath and told myself that whatever happened, I would survive it.

"I wanted to talk to you." My feet got caught up with each other, and I stumbled, but Jase was there to keep me from eating grass.

Color stained my cheeks. I had all this power, and I still tripped over my own damn feet. I sure as hell didn't expect my body to start tingling. My tattoos shifted and moved on my skin, that now glimmered like a rainbow on the surface of the sea.

The four of them stopped walking, most likely for my own safety. "What took you so long?" Zade replied, slipping a hand under my elbow, his eyes bright with delightful humor.

Kieran was at my other side, a hand at the small of my back. "We've been going crazy waiting for you to figure out what you wanted."

What? All this time they were waiting for me?

I couldn't decide who to look at because they were all equally important, so I kept my gaze centered on my twining fingers. "That's the thing... I don't know what I want, except the four of you. I don't know how to be a queen, or what is expected of me."

Issik slipped a finger under my chin, tipping my face upward to meet his gaze. "We won't abandon you. Not ever." The expression I saw there had my heart squeezing.

Zade's hand slid down my arm to entwine our fingers. "We're forever in your debt."

"Veil Isles will only have one queen," Jase offered softly. "That is, if she will have us—all of us."

"I don't understand." My brows scrunched.

Kieran looked into my eyes, into my very soul. "None of us are willing to live without you, or to let the other make you his queen, so we've decided it's time for a new era, and it is only fitting that the one who saved us becomes the Isles' one queen—the queen of the Veil."

My legs wobbled. I hadn't gotten used to having my own kingdom yet, and now they wanted me to rule over the continent. I was young and inexperienced. What kind of queen would I make?

"What about having an heir?" It was the only way they could ensure the dragon line didn't die. With the curse broken, they could once again mate and have children.

"Our relationship might be unconventional, but we have a proposal for you," Jase explained. The four of them looked at each other before turning those vibrant eyes to me. "You share the power of five dragon stones, making you the ideal mate. Our sons and daughters will be stronger."

Zade brushed a thumb across my cheek, leaving a trail of warmth behind. "We only ask that you spend equal time between our kingdoms and their people, including yours. You will help us rule the courts of the Veil."

It was too good to be true. I wanted to throw myself into each one of their arms. My joy and relief overwhelmed me.

"This is ultimately your choice, and it isn't all or nothing, but we're all in agreement on what we want," Issik confirmed.

Tears of pure happiness glistened in my eyes, of belonging, of love—a well of emotions. "I've never wanted anything more."

"We'll make you happy," Jase promised.

"I know."

A disarming grin hooked the corners of Kieran's lips. "So, whose kingdom is first?"

Here we go again.

I laughed as the arguing of the four descendants broke out in my gardens. Some things never changed, and I wouldn't have it any other way. My chest bloomed with unconditional love for these four dragons.

To be Continued...

Thank you so much for joining me on this journey

into the lives of the dragon descendants. I fell so much in love with these characters and will miss them dearly. Hopefully, I gave them a happily-ever-after that fantasies are made of. I ventured into new territory when I decided to write a reverse harem, and I hope I did it justice.

DRAGON DESCENDANTS

A REVERSE HAREM SERIES

A NOTE FROM THE AUTHOR

Thank you so much for reading Thawing Frost, Dragon Descendants, book 4.

I truly hope you have enjoyed reading it, if you have, please show your support by leaving a review. It only takes few moments, visit my Amazon Author page:

J.L. Weil
https://amzn.to/2OPz6J3

For the latest news about new releases, sales, upcoming books, giveaways, and more join my news letter today!
http://www.jlweil.com/vip-readers

DRAGON DESCENDANTS

A REVERSE HAREM SERIES

ABOUT THE AUTHOR

USA TODAY Bestselling author J.L. Weil lives in Illinois where she writes Teen & New Adult Paranormal Romances about spunky, smart mouth girls who always wind up in dire situations. For every sassy girl, there is an equally mouthwatering, overprotective guy. Of course, there is lots of kissing. And stuff.

An admitted addict to Love Pink clothes, raspberry mochas from Starbucks, and Jensen Ackles. She loves gushing about books and Supernatural with her readers. She is the author of the International Bestselling Raven & Divisa series.

Don't forget to follow her!

www.jlweil.com
www.facebook.com/jenniferlweil
www.twitter.com/JLWeil
www.instagram.com/jlweil

Made in the USA
Columbia, SC
04 May 2022